Stalker

Stalker

Brenda Hampton

www.urbanbooks.net

Urban Books, LLC
300 Farmingdale Road, NY-Route 109
Farmingdale, NY 11735

ISBN 13: 978-1-62286-671-7
ISBN 10: 1-62286-671-1

First Mass Market Printing January 2018
First Trade Paperback Printing March 2017
Printed in the United States of America

10 9 8 7 6 5 4 3 2 1

*This is a work of fiction. Any references or similar-
ities to actual events, real people, living or dead, or
to real locales are intended to give the novel a sense
of reali_y. Any similarity in other names, charac-
ters, pl____ __ __ __li__ __ __tirely coincidental.*

Distrib_____ __ __ __sington Publishing Corp.
Submit _rders to:
Custom
400 H___n Road
Westm_____
Phone:
Fax: 1-

Chapter One

Sometimes, life was so unfair, but I just had to go with the flow. I had been trying to get my ducks in a row for a very long time. I *thought* my husband and I would be together forever. *Thought* he would do right by our daughter. *Thought* he would help me take care of her, and I never predicted that after our divorce he would abandon both of us. I had no problem with him not reaching out to me, but what about our daughter, Kendal? She didn't deserve the ill treatment from Malik. Shame on him for thinking that his fifteen-year-old child didn't need him.

I'd had plenty of conversations with Kendal about her father. At first, she didn't understand what kind of man he was. She loved him with every fiber of her being, but it wasn't long before he started to show his true colors. Kendal noticed the horrible way he spoke to me, the ongoing disrespect and drinking habits that had become unbearable. There were times when he was so drunk that he claimed he couldn't make it home. He always made excuses for not being home, but after I followed him one day and discovered what he had been doing on some of those late nights, I decided to wash my hands of our marriage.

Given the fact that he had lost his job, we often struggled. I had to pick up extra hours at work, but never in my wildest dream did I think Malik's answer would be to sell drugs. I couldn't believe his mind-set. When I questioned why he thought that was the only route to go, he stuck to his guns, saying that he wasn't going to stop. He was willing to put our lives at risk. That was a big no-no for me. I worked too darn hard for what we had—I wasn't about to allow anyone to come into my home, arrest me, and take everything. Malik didn't see it my way. All he wanted was dirty money that would be a true setback for us. I had known him since high school, and it hurt me to the core when our marriage came to an end. The drinking was already enough, but the drug selling I just couldn't do.

From that moment on, I vowed to never put that much time and energy into another man again; promised myself that it would be just

Kendal and me. She was my everything, even though she was starting to become a force to be reckoned with. Nonetheless, I understood her somewhat reckless behavior. She had been acting out because of Malik. She had also been a little jealous of my new relationship with Brent Carson, a man who made me change my thought process about dating again. He gave me hope.

The day I met him, I was completely down in the dumps. The principal at Kendal's school had called to tell me she had been suspended for fighting. I was livid, and right after I picked her up from school, we stopped at the grocery store. I couldn't stop fussing at Kendal about her actions, and as we loaded bags into the trunk of the car, Brent approached us. Thinking back to that day, I sat on the edge of my bed, reminiscing about a turning point in my life.

"She was the one who started it," Kendal *hissed while shoving a bag into the trunk. "You weren't there, so for you to be so upset with me is ridiculous, especially when you're the one who always told me to defend myself."*

"Yes, I did tell you that, but defending yourself doesn't mean that you have to go around fighting everyone because they say things about you that you don't like. Learn to brush off some of that mess and keep it moving."

"I tried, but she kept getting in my face. When she spit on me, that's when I punched her."

I sighed and rolled my eyes at Kendal. This was the third time she had been suspended. While I knew there were mean girls at her school, I also knew that Kendal didn't know how to control herself. She would flip out if someone didn't like what she wore or if they said something about her appearance. I had a feeling that these incidents were more about Kendal than they were about the other students picking on her.

"We'll talk more about this when we get home, young lady. You've already embarrassed me enough."

"You're embarrassing yourself." Exemplifying much attitude, her neck rolled in circles. "And you didn't have to put my business out there in a grocery store. People were shaking their heads at you, not me."

Maybe they were, but I surely didn't give a damn. When or wherever I had something to say, I was going to say it.

"I have no problem speaking my mind, and I'm going to continue to do so right now. Wipe that frown off your face, lower your tone, remove the case of soda from the cart, and do not throw any more bags into my trunk."

Kendal growled as she picked up the case of soda, carefully putting it in the trunk as she was told. I was just about ready to close it when a man approached us with a smile on his face.

"Hello, ladies." He looked directly at me. "I don't mean to interrupt, but I was standing over there by my car when I heard the two of you arguing. I also heard a little back-and-forth while I was in the store. I wanted to say something then. I don't know what could cause the two of you to speak to each other this way, but it's not a good look. Everything can be worked out, and harsh words can leave lifetime scars. I often tell my students how important it is for them to respect their parents, and as parents, we also have to respect our children."

Kendal and I both stood stunned, wondering why this man had poked his nose in our business. All Kendal did was cross her arms and narrow her eyes at him. I was the one who spoke up.

"I apologize if our little disagreement disturbed you, but when all is said and done, we do respect each other. I just had a few things that I needed to get off my chest. I guess she did too. Now, if you don't mind, we need to get back to our business."

"Sure. And like I said, I didn't mean to pry."

"I don't recall you saying that you didn't mean to pry. Maybe I didn't hear it."

He nodded as he wiped across his Tyson Beckford thick lips that made me switch my thoughts to how sexy he was. His cologne was doing quite a number on me too, but I was so engulfed in his rudeness that I had to push his handsomeness aside. He continued to smile, even though I wasn't. Neither was Kendal.

"Are you sure I didn't say that?" he asked.

"Positive. What you said was, you didn't mean to interrupt us."

He snapped his fingers. "Yes, you would be correct. I did say that, and I apologize for getting it wrong."

His apology caused me to soften my tone. "No big deal, okay? We all make mistakes sometimes. I guess that arguing with my daughter in public isn't exactly a good idea."

"No, it's not, but I'm not judging you at all. It's easy for our kids, especially teenagers, to get underneath our skin."

Both of our eyes shifted to Kendal. She released a deep sigh before opening the door to get in the car. After she closed the door, I turned my attention back to the man who held my attention for more than five minutes. That was rare.

"What did you say your name was?" My eyes scanned him from head to toe. Nice shoes, no ring, neat clothing, trimmed goatee, luscious brown skin, and those lips—I was sure they worked wonders. If I had one complaint, that would be his size. He was a bit thicker than I preferred, and I had never dated a bald-headed man. But there was something about him . . . maybe those almond-shaped eyes that screamed Morris Chestnut.

"Sorry again," he said, chuckling and extending his hand to mine. "I guess I forgot to tell you that too. My name is Brent. Brent Carson."

My frown had converted into a smile as I shook his hand. "Abigail, but my friends call me Abby."

"Nice to meet you, Abby. Since I've made a few mistakes referring to my approach, may I offer you something else, other than an apology?"

I shrugged and released his hand. "Sure. Why not?"

"How about dinner? Your choice, and you say when."

My smile had gotten wider. "Okay. How about you give me your number, and I'll give you a call whenever I'm ready?"

He wasted no time slipping his hand in his pocket, handing me a business card. "Here *you go. Call whenever you're ready. Hopefully, soon."*

I dropped the card into my purse before encouraging him to have a good day. He told me to do the same, and almost a week later, I reached out to him for dinner. That was a year ago. Since then, Brent and I had spent almost every day together. We were a happy couple. I never imagined myself being this enthused about a relationship again. Brent was everything. He had it all from A to Z, and I was so thankful that he had come into my life at a time when I was so broken. He proved to me that there were still good men in this world, ones who listened to a woman's wants and needs. Men who knew how to treat women, who didn't mind going out of their way for them, and who took charge of the relationship.

Just last month, he took me on a surprise vacation to Jamaica. We had the time of our lives. I was still trying to come down from my high. I had definitely fallen in love with him, and even though I hadn't said those words to him, he knew how I felt. The way I looked at him said so. The things I'd done for him confirmed my deep love for him. I'll be the first to admit that it was rare for me to drop down on my knees and give a man head. I had only gone there with my ex-husband a few times, but with Brent, I surely didn't mind. Not after the way he pleased me. He was so good to me sexually, it was a pleasure to finally have sex with someone for more than ten minutes. That was all Malik ever gave me. Ten long and boring minutes, and then it was over. He never caressed my body, rubbed my feet, ran my bathwater . . . Brent, on the other hand, did it all.

While still on the edge of the bed, I tied my tennis shoes, already knowing that I was running late for my date with Brent. My sweat suit was on and my hair was in an asymmetrical pixie cut that was shaved on one side. Even though Brent said we weren't going anywhere special for our one-year anniversary, I still dolled myself up. My makeup was flawless, eyelashes were thick and full, and my light-brown skin glowed. I always made sure my appearance was on point, and no one would ever catch me in a grocery store, or even going outside to get the mail, looking a hot mess. Brent complimented how well I took care of myself—I guess my "me first" motto was finally appreciated.

In a rush to meet Brent at his place before one o'clock, I hurried around my bedroom, looking for my car keys. I thought I'd laid them on my nightstand, but there was a possibility that Kendal had removed them. I figured she was in her bedroom, so I made my way down the hallway, yelling out to her.

"What?" she answered with an attitude. "Why are you yelling my name?"

I stood in her doorway and saw her sitting in front of the computer with headphones around her neck.

"Have you seen my keys?"

"No, I have not. Besides, what would I be doing with your keys? I don't even drive yet."

"Yes, you do. You have had my car before. And even if you've been taking it to learn how to drive, all you have to do is ask. I told you before that I don't mind you taking—"

She cut me off. "I said, I don't have your keys. I've also never driven your car. Tammi is the only person who let me drive her car before."

"Tammi? Tammi doesn't even have insurance on that raggedy car she has. You'd better not be driving her car. Has she even turned sixteen yet?"

"Yes, Mama. I told you that about two months ago. I guess you weren't paying attention."

Every time I was on my way out with Brent, Kendal caught an attitude. I wasn't going to let her ruin this special day for me, so I kept her comment about me not paying attention to her to myself.

"In case you forgot, I'm going to an amusement park with Brent. The offer still stands. You and Tammi can come along as well, but if you change your mind, you'll need to be ready in about ten or fifteen minutes."

Kendal pursed her lips, then picked up a brush from her desk. She brushed her long hair into a ponytail before securing it with a rubber band.

"I'm not interested in going to an amusement park. I'm surprised that you're going, especially at your age. Amusement parks are for kids."

I cocked my head back in surprise. "Amusement parks are for people who like to have fun. And I may be a thirty-six-year-old, wrinkled woman in your eyes, but my life isn't over until I'm dead and in my grave. You're just jealous because everyone thinks we're sisters. That, my dear child, is because you have a mother who loves herself and makes herself the priority."

"That may be somewhat true, but you look like that because black don't crack. As for the sister thing, my friends just don't know any better."

We both laughed.

"Your friends know better than you do, so stop being a hater. Meanwhile, are you going with me? I know you said you're not interested, but I don't want you to stay cooped up in here and on that computer all day."

"I'm fine. Go have fun with you know who. You know if you're late, he's going to be ringing my cell phone looking for you."

"He hasn't called your phone, has he?"

"Yes. About three or four times. I don't even know how he got my number, but please tell him how inappropriate it is for him to be calling me, looking for you."

"I didn't know he had your number either, but don't be so mean about it. I don't know why you don't like Brent. He's always been kind to you, and it was very nice of him to buy you that watch you wanted."

Kendal winced. "I didn't ask him to buy me anything. You probably told him to buy it, just to get on my good side. He can spend all the money he wants. I still don't like him. Never have, never will."

It disappointed me to hear Kendal speak that way about Brent, especially since he had put forth so much effort to let her know how much he cared about both of us.

"I assume you feel that way about him because of your dad. But get over it, Kendal, because he and I will never, ever get back together. I don't know why you would think—"

"This has nothing to do with him. I just don't like Brent. Right from the beginning, he rubbed me the wrong way. What kind of man comes up to you on a parking lot to tell you how to conduct yourself with your own child? Gimmie a break. There are multiple things about him I don't like, but as long as you like him, who cares what I think?"

I walked into Kendal's room and stood in front of her. "I care, but I just don't understand why you're so hard on him."

"I already told you a million and one times. He's fake, he's sneaky, he's bossy, he's a liar— need I say more?"

"You've said all of those things before, but there's nothing to back all of that up. That's why I know this is about Malik. I'm sorry that he's not in our lives anymore, but I'm glad that I made the right decision to move on from him. I hope you understand why, and you're not upset with me because he isn't around anymore."

Kendal released a deep sigh. "Believe me, I couldn't care less about that man. I don't care about Brent either, and for the last time, I'm not interested in being at an amusement park with a fake man who is trying too hard to get me on his team."

"Well, as long as you stay on my team, that's all that's matters. Now, don't stay up too late. If you decide to leave the house, call my cell phone to let me know where you're going."

"Tammi may come over later, but that's it. Have fun and keep your eyes on the creep."

I ignored Kendal's comment. She always had something negative to say. No matter who I dated, she wouldn't like them. Her feelings were exactly the same as mine when my mother divorced my father and remarried. I hated my stepfather, but after several years had passed, he wound up being the best thing that happened to my mother and to me.

My keys were on the kitchen table, right next to my purse. I told Kendal good-bye, and almost thirty minutes later, I arrived at Brent's house in Clayton, Missouri. Clayton was an upscale neighborhood on the outskirts of St. Louis. But the houses, lofts, and apartments were over-priced. Brent lived in a ranch-style, brick house that was well kept and clean. The lawn was well manicured and the three-bedroom house sat on a tiny hill with a garage several feet behind it.

His car was parked in the gravel-paved driveway, and after I parked my car behind it, I went to the door and rang the doorbell.

No one came to the door, but as I opened the screen to knock, I saw a note on the door that said: *Open*. I turned the knob, and as the door came open, I saw a trail of red, long-stemmed roses, leading to the dining room. When I reached the dining room, the trail of roses continued through the kitchen and all the way to the cozy den where we often chilled and watched TV. This time, however, the TV was not on. The drapes were closed, and numerous scented candles lit up the space. Two portable massage beds were side by side, along with fluffy pillows on top for comfort. Brent was lying on his stomach, with a masseuse standing next to him. A smile was on her face, and as she rubbed her oily hands together, she nudged her head toward the other bed that had a rose on top of it.

"We thought you'd never get here," she said. "Mr. Carson was just getting ready to call you."

Brent sat up, then laid a white towel across his lap. "I figured you would be late, but I'm glad you're here. Happy Anniversary, baby. Sorry we won't be able to make it to the amusement park, but I don't think you'll mind because I have an amazing day planned for us. For starters, you'll

have to remove your clothes. Either in here or
feel free to use the bathroom."

I was totally surprised by all of this. My mouth
dropped wide open. The cozy room felt like a
spa, and the smell of many sweet fragrances
infused the air. I could tell the Chinese woman
was a professional, simply because her skin
appeared so rich and smooth. And the way she
had everything set up let me know she had been
at this for quite some time. As for me, I didn't
mind getting naked. I had a model-like figure
with curves in all the right places. Brent had
seen me naked plenty of times before, and I was
so sure that my nakedness wouldn't be a big deal
to the masseuse.

"I'm fine right here," I said to Brent while
removing my tennis shoes. "But you didn't
have to do this. I seriously thought we were
going to an amusement park. I was looking forward to getting on a roller coaster and hearing
you scream like a little girl at the top of your
lungs."

Brent laughed. "We'll go some other time so
I can hear you scream at the top of your lungs.
Maybe next weekend, just not today. Today is
special. Real special."

I wasn't going to dispute that. This day was
special. He was so amazing, and no one had ever
surprised me like this before. Brent watched as I

started to remove my sweat suit. The masseuse was now a few feet away from him with her back facing us. A towel was thrown over her shoulder. I saw her pick up a bottle and sniff the cream. She squeezed a portion in her hand before rubbing both hands together. As she worked on her magic potion, I was now down to my burgundy silk bra and panties. My breasts were firm, but small. Stomach was flat, hips were wide, and ass was just right. I looked fabulous in almost everything I wore, and when a compliment came from behind me, I swung around to see who it was. There stood a gay man with his hair as straight as mine. His hair, however, flowed midway down his back. The makeup he wore was near perfection, and his ruby-red lips were pursed.

"Girl, that booty is muaaah. You got that hourglass thingy going on. I take it that 'fit' is your middle name."

I appreciated his kind words, especially since I worked out faithfully to keep myself feeling good and looking young. All I could do was thank the man, even though I hadn't a clue who he was or why he was there.

"You're so welcome, sweetie," he said, marching into the room. "Now, go lie down and allow me to make you feel and look even better than you do right now."

Of course, I was a little skeptical about this, but I didn't think that Brent would put me in a situation that he was uncomfortable with. Before I even made it to the bed, he reached out his hand for me to take it.

"My friend, Jeff, can be a bit blunt at times, but he is going to make you feel like a new woman. I'll be right here, holding your hand and looking into those beautiful eyes I've been thinking about all day."

I blushed as Brent pulled my body close to his. He was fully naked, but the towel remained across his lap. I planted a soft kiss on his lips, but when his tongue slipped into my mouth, we indulged in a lengthy kiss, as if no one else was in the room with us.

"Get it," Jeff said, clapping his hands and smacking his lips. "As Nelly ol' fine self says, 'It's already gettin' real hot in herrre.' I suggest y'all put that lip smacking on hold for now, because Lucy and I do not want to be in this room when wet panties start flying."

Brent and I backed away from the intense kiss. He looked at Jeff and shook his head.

"Jeff, keep the jokes to a minimum, all right? I want you to get down to business and show my beautiful woman why you are considered one of the best in the business." He looked at Lucy and smiled. "No offense, Lucy."

She shrugged her shoulders. "None taken, because you have the best in the business working on you today. Jeff can't touch what I do. That's why he talks too much. He wants his customers to get distracted by his god-awful jokes."

Jeff snapped his fingers, then put his hand on his hip. "Chile, the only thing you can do better than me is fry some rice and make hot braised chicken. As for this masseur thing, I got it on lock. Brent was not mistaken. He knows who to call when he wants the best. So, come here, Sweet Pea. Remove those silky panties and that bra, and let me show you why I am King of the Masseurs. After I'm done, you will be compelled to bow down to me, as Lucy has done in the past."

Lucy giggled and remained silent. I looked at Brent. He gave me a nod. I don't know why, but I felt as if this would be an unforgettable day and night.

Jeff pranced over to where Lucy was to prepare his magic potion as well. I removed my bra and panties, and after lying on my stomach, I covered my bottom half with a clean white sheet. Brent was on his stomach too. He reached for my hand again.

"Are you hungry?" he asked.

"No, not really. I'm still kind of full from breakfast. I made omelets for Kendal and me. They were delicious and were filled with lots of meat."

"If it was anything like the one you made me a few weeks back, yes, you should be full. Hopefully not too full, because I am going to throw down on dinner for you tonight."

Brent could cook, so I was getting more and more excited. "Care to give me any hints?"

"Nope. My lips are sealed. Just think seafood and you'll know where I'm going."

"It sounds good already. Maybe there will be enough leftovers for me to take Kendal a plate. I doubt that she will get up and cook herself something to eat."

"If she gets hungry, she'll eat. How is she doing anyway?"

"She's okay. We had a little disagreement before I left, but that's becoming the norm in our household."

"Well, remember that you're the adult and she's the child. Kendal tries to play on your intelligence sometimes. She's a smart girl, and she tries to get underneath your skin on purpose. Other than that, you have a beautiful daughter who should be praised for being an A student. I wish my students were like her."

I wouldn't dare tell Brent how Kendal truly felt about him, so I switched the subject back to dinner. I was looking forward to it, as well as to anything else he had up his sleeve. He had already topped my one-year anniversary with Malik. He was so darn drunk that he wound up passed out on the couch with vomit on his shirt. We argued the whole day, and, eventually, I left to go shopping. Thinking about him almost ruined the moment. I turned my thoughts back to Brent who had asked Lucy to turn up the soothing jazz music.

"Just a little," he said. "Thanks, and I think we're ready for the two of you now."

Jeff strutted over to me with a basket that had oils, creams, and sprays in it.

"Sweet Pea, just close your eyes and relax. I promise that I won't touch anything private, but you must know that your luscious little booty got me thinking about something that—"

"Jeff," Brent warned. "Don't go there, man. I don't want you speaking to my woman like that. You're making her real uncomfortable."

Jeff flicked his brows and looked at me. "Sweet Pea, am I making you uncomfortable? If I am, please tell me now and I will zip my pretty lips."

"I'm not uncomfortable, but I would like for you to stop all the chitchatting and show me why you're considered the King of Masseurs. That's all I really care about, because the way Lucy is over there working on Brent, it looks to me as if she is really king."

Jeff put me in my place. "Okay, see, now you done started something. I refuse to have you thinking that way, so let me hush my mouth and get down to the real business at hand."

Within ten minutes, he made me feel as if I had died and gone to heaven. His hands added the perfect amount of pressure to my body. My eyelids kept fluttering. It felt like I was being hypnotized. Whatever he massaged my body with smelled like coconuts. And with the ceiling fan delivering a cool breeze, all I needed was sand and water to make me feel as if I was on an island.

"Jeff, I think Sweet Pea is enjoying this," Brent said. "She won't even open her eyes and talk to me."

"That's because I'm falling asleep," I moaned. "This feels soooo good, and his hands . . . His hands are everything."

"So, what are you saying? His hands feel better than mine?"

"Sweet Pea, don't answer that because he is only going to get his feelings hurt. You know damn well these hands feel better than those rough ones you got. But, girl, go ahead and lie if you must."

"I can't lie," I confessed. "You are the king, Jeff. Brent, however, is the master."

Brent laughed. "I'll take what I can get. Thanks."

I went back into a coma as Jeff scrolled his hands down my back, traveling south. He worked wonders on my legs and thighs. I didn't mind that he occasionally touched my cheeks.

"Be careful with those," Brent mumbled as Lucy had him in a trance too. "And don't get too happy."

"I'll try not to, but chile, if this buttocks belonged to my man—"

"Don't even go there," Brent said. "We got your point."

I blushed and kept my mind focused on the king delivering exactly what he had promised. And when all was said and done, I was sad that my session had come to an end.

"Wipe those tears, Sweet Pea. I'm going to leave you my contact information. If you ever want to visit the Virgin Islands again, just call me, and I'll come running."

"I need to go there once a week, so please leave your card on the bed. And thank you so much. I really needed that."

"Don't thank me. Thank your man because this is going to set him back a pretty penny. I come, but I don't come cheap."

Brent laughed as he watched Lucy and Jeff pack up their belongings to go. I wasn't sure how much he'd forked out for this, but it was very worth it. I gave them both tips, but they refused to take it.

"Everything is already taken care of, Sweet Pea," Jeff said, air-kissing my cheeks. "Have a nice evening and don't let Brent get you all sweaty and sticky right away. Try to hold off on the goodies until later. But if you can't wait, I truly understand."

Brent shoved Jeff toward the door. And after Lucy said good-bye to me, Brent walked both of them to the door with a towel wrapped around his waist. His facial features reminded me so much of Morris Chestnut, but body-wise, he wasn't stacked with muscles. It didn't bother me one bit, and I was surprised when he started working out with me a few months ago. Within two weeks, he'd lost almost ten pounds. He was down to 210, but he told me his goal was 200. Tonight, I would definitely help him reach his goal by offering a little sexual exercise.

Brent came back into the den, looking directly at me. I was still sitting on the bed with the sheet wrapped around me.

"Dinner now or later," he said, walking in my direction. He stood between my legs with his arms tightened around my waist.

"Hmmm, let's see. If we don't get started on dinner now, what else do you have in mind?"

"A whole lot, but for now, how about another one of those juicy kisses you always give me."

"I can definitely handle that."

I leaned in to give Brent a kiss. Our hands started to roam, and after I removed the towel from his waist, he made the sheet from around me disappear. I stood, just to get a feel of his body pressed against mine. My breasts were smashed against his chest, and with a chunk of my ass in his hands, things started to get heated.

"Let . . . Let's wait," he said, backing away from my lips. "Let's go to the kitchen so you can help me cook. I love when you help me cook, especially when you're naked."

"I don't mind, but I thought you were supposed to cook me dinner. All I wanted to do is watch."

He lifted my hand, kissing the back of it. "You can do that too, but I need your help with the salad. I love the one you made for my lunch that day. It was gone in less than five minutes."

I agreed to make the salad, and as we made our way to the kitchen with no clothes on, Brent cranked up the music. We danced a little and couldn't stop talking about crazy Jeff while we prepared the food. Brent was in the process of making some grilled shrimp, and I was standing by the counter, chopping lettuce for the salad.

"I didn't know what to think of him," I said. "But he is so talented with his hands that I didn't care how blunt he was."

Brent turned off the stove and came over to me. He stood behind me with his arms secured around my waist.

"Do you really want to talk about talented hands? I can show you a man with talented hands right now."

I picked up a leaf of lettuce, popping it into his mouth. He chewed, then lightly bit into the side of my neck. His hands covered my breasts, and as he massaged them together, I closed my eyes. I was so in love with Brent, but I just didn't know how to say it. More than anything, I wanted him to tell me first. In due time, I assumed that he would say it. I didn't want to push. This felt so right, and my gut told me that, one day, he would ask me to be his wife. I was ready to be a married woman again. Brent proved to me that we could do this. We got along well, and thus far, we'd had very few disagreements. Arguments never happened between us, and that was because Brent listened to any concerns that I'd had. I guessed with him being a high school teacher, nothing really fazed him. His students gave him hell, but Brent knew how to turn every situation to good, just as he had done with my thoughts of never dating again.

"How do these hands feel now?" He whispered in my ear as his hand was cuffed over my pussy. His middle finger was dipped into my insides, stirring my juices. "Am I talented too?"

"Very. Because any man who can make me rain on his finger like you are has major skills."

Brent added another finger to the mix, causing me to make the right decision and put dinner on hold. I bent over, and the only thing being served to me, in the moment, was his satisfying dick that made my legs weaken every time he thrusted forward. He held my waist, and as his goods hit the tip of my hotspot, I expressed my enthusiasm for the man in my life.

"Happy Anniversary, baby!" I shouted. "Thank you for everything, especially for giving me this . . . this orgasm I'm about tooooo—"

I couldn't finish the sentence, but he already knew what was coming next. He released his energy with me, and as we dropped to the floor, we quickly cuddled in each other's arms. Brent planted a delicate kiss on my sweaty forehead.

"Happy Anniversary to you too," he said. "And many more to come."

I nodded, certainly in agreement with that.

Chapter Two

It had been a long day. The customers at the retail chain I worked for had been working my nerves. There was a 50 percent off everything sale, but for some people, 50 percent wasn't enough. One lady chewed me out about not being able to use her coupon.

"Ma'am, if I honor your 50-percent-off coupon, that would make the item free. Our store is in no position to give away merchandise for free."

"First of all, this isn't your store," the snippy old woman said. "You just work here, and I doubt that you own any stock in this place. This is bullshit, and I want to speak to the manager, now. I should be able to use this coupon without any questions asked."

Lord knows I wanted to go off on this woman who had spit sprinkles flying from her mouth. But in my position, I had to conduct myself with as much professionalism as possible.

I replied with a smile. "I *am* the store manager, and there is no one else on duty for you to
speak to. If you would like to speak to someone
at our corporate office about the policy per-
taining to coupons, I'll be happy to give you a
number to call."

"Please do. This is ridiculous, and I've seen
other people using their coupons today."

I remained silent as many people in the
long lines watched the disrespectful exchange
between the woman and me. She snatched the
coupon from my hand and had the audacity to
call me a "stupid bitch" as she walked off. I continued to smile at her, as well as at the customers
who looked at me, shaking their heads. Some of
the stares were probably because the long lines
hadn't moved much. But with a sale like today,
there wasn't much that I could do about it.

Feeling frustrated about the incident and getting real tired of people's shit, I went through the
employees-only entrance and started snatching
clothes that needed to be tagged off the racks. I
threw them in a pile, and when I almost tripped
over a heavy jacket on the floor, I kicked it away
from me. I gathered several broken hangers that
were on the floor too, growling as I trashed them.
The only thing that calmed me down was when
one of my coworkers came in the back, looking

for a pair of shoes in a particular size. My mood changed fast.

"I haven't seen any more of those shoes back here, but you can go check. Another customer inquired the other day about the same shoes, and I remember looking for them."

"Okay," she said. "Thanks, hon. You're a doll."

"Yes, I am. I'm glad someone noticed."

A few hours later, things had completely calmed down. I was in my office, looking over an inventory listing that was nearly ten pages. When I heard someone clear their throat, I looked up and saw Brent standing in the doorway. A bundle of roses was in his hand, and the warm smile on his face made me feel a whole lot better.

"Rough day at work?" he said, then came into my office.

"That would be putting it mildly. Only two hours left and this sale will be over."

Brent laughed as he laid the flowers on my desk. "You forgot to get these off the floor the other night. I didn't want them to die, so I gathered up some to bring to you."

"Awww, that's so sweet of you. And I wouldn't have forgotten them had you not occupied my mind with other things."

He came over to my side of the desk to give me a kiss. "For the record, you had my mind occupied too. Can't stop thinking about what you put on me. If I wasn't leaving to go out of town this evening, I would definitely invite you over for another meal."

I put a frown on my face. "Sorry to hear that you'll be gone again. Where to now?"

"Another teacher's convention. I'll be back in less than a week, hopefully sooner."

"What exactly am I supposed to do with myself while you're away?"

"I'm sure you'll think of something to keep you busy. If not, you can always skype with me in the evenings. My schedule is pretty packed during the day."

"Well, skyping will just have to do. As for now, I need to take advantage of you while I can."

Brent welcomed the idea, and before he left my office, we toyed around with each other in another office in the far back. No sex, just teased each other. I gave him a juicy kiss before walking him to the door to exit.

"Safe travels," I said. "And thanks for the flowers."

"Anytime, baby. Stay sexy and I'll see you soon."

I watched Brent as he opened the door to his car and sped off. When I returned to my office, one of my coworkers was standing by my desk, sniffing my flowers.

"You, my dear, are so lucky. Not only do you have a good-looking man, but he's super romantic too, isn't he?"

"Very much so. I'm definitely going to miss him for the next few days."

"At least you won't be tied up in here. You're only on the schedule for three days next week. That should give you a little time to relax and forget about those grumpy customers who wouldn't know what the word respect means, even if it slaps them in the face."

All I could do was laugh. I was in such a good mood. I had Brent to thank for that.

Three hours later, I was finally at home. I expected Kendal to be there, but when I went to her room, she was gone. It was a Friday night. I figured she must've gotten into something with Tammi. I called Kendal's cell phone, just to make sure everything was good. She didn't answer so I left a message for her to call me back ASAP, and I sent a text message as well. I headed to my bedroom, slipped into my pajamas, then returned to the kitchen to pour a glass of wine. There wasn't much to watch on TV, so I grabbed a book I'd been reading and stayed up for the next few hours reading. I was curious to know if Brent had made it to his destination, but just as I was getting ready to call him, Kendal called.

"Where are you?" I asked. "It's getting late, and you should have let me know where you would be."

"If you check your messages, maybe you'll hear the one I left you. I told you I was at Tammi's house. If you don't mind, can I spend the night at her house?"

I wanted to say no, but with all that had been going on with Kendal, she needed time away with friends to enjoy herself.

"I don't mind. Just be here by six o'clock tomorrow evening. I'm going to the Soulard Market in the morning to get some fruit and vegetables. I also need to stop at the grocery store. Do you want anything?"

"Just some cherries and Fruit Loops. That's it."

"Okay. Tell Tammi I said hello. I'll see you tomorrow."

I ended my call with Kendal, then called Brent. I was totally shocked when a woman answered his phone.

"I . . . I'm sorry, but I must have the wrong number. Is this, uh, Brent Carson's phone?"

The woman hung up on me. I sat up in bed with a twisted face while punching his number into my cell phone. This time, no one answered. I didn't bother to leave a message, but I waited a few more minutes before calling again. There was still no answer, and by now, my blood was starting to boil. *Who in the hell was that answering his phone? Did I have the wrong number?* I surely didn't think so, but there had to be some kind of explanation for this. Unfortunately for me, an explanation didn't come until almost one o'clock in the morning. I was still wide awake, fuming inside because it had taken Brent this long to call me back.

"This better be good," I said in a snippy tone. "I can't believe it took you until one in the morning to call back."

"I apologize, but I lost my phone earlier. Another one of the teachers found it and brought it to my room. I saw that you'd called, and I didn't want to wait until morning to call you back."

It sounded like a good explanation, but why did the heifer hang up on me? Maybe she didn't want Brent to know she had answered his phone.

"Thanks for calling, but I'm going back to sleep now. I'm glad you got everything worked out with your phone because whoever answered it hung up on me."

"Her name was Deena. She told me someone had called, but she said my battery died and she didn't get a chance to ask who you were. I'm just glad that I didn't lose my phone. That would have been devastating because all of my contacts are in there. Not to mention those sexy pictures I have of you."

He was charming, but I wasn't moved. I wasn't sure if he sensed my attitude or not, but truthfully, I wasn't in the mood to talk right now. I had been up for hours, concerned about why another woman had answered his phone. And even though his explanation sounded legit, it still didn't help to calm me.

"I can't imagine losing my phone either, but things do happen. Meanwhile, I'll give you a call tomorrow. I'm real sleepy, and I can't stay up much longer."

"Okay, sweetheart. Get some rest and I'll give you a holler tomorrow."

I replied, "Sure," then ended the call.

Something didn't feel right about the phone incident. I didn't think, or at least I hoped, that Brent wouldn't lie to me. Thus far, he appeared to be a very honest man. The last time he was out of town, we had no issues whatsoever with his phone. I finally fell asleep, thinking that maybe it was just me.

The following morning, I felt a little more upbeat. I went to the basement to work out on my treadmill, and after kicking up a sweat, I showered and put on some clothes. Keeping it simple, I had on a pair of tight-fitting, tan-colored capris and a pink ribbed tank shirt. My haircut looked as if I'd just left the beautician, and with little makeup on, I headed to the Soulard Market.

As usual, the place was packed with Saturday morning shoppers who wanted to get real discounts on produce. I could barely find a place to park, but I finally lucked up on a parking spot that was several feet away from the door. As people browsed around and a band played jazz music outdoors, I waited in a short line to get a creamy ice-cream cone. A man in front of me claimed he had lost his money and didn't have enough to pay. He held up the line, and the woman at the ice-cream stand wasn't nice about it at all.

"Sir, you've been up here three times already. Obviously, you don't have any money, so would you mind moving aside so I can take care of the lady behind you?"

The man pivoted to look at me. His light brown eyes got real wide, and he cracked a smile, showing his pearly white teeth. I assumed the man was homeless, and even though his beautiful wavy hair was dusty, I predicted that once upon a time, it probably looked good. His frame was pretty cut too, but the raggedy clothes kind of confirmed his status.

"Listen," he said with a scraggly voice. He cleared his throat to speak. "If you need me to do some work for you around your house, let me know. I can also wash your car or hold your grocery bags for you too. I'm a li'l short on change. I was just trying to get an ice-cream cone and a sandwich for later."

There were plenty of homeless people lurking around in downtown St. Louis, but nobody ever asked me for anything. I didn't mind digging into my purse to help the man out. He was all smiles when I paid the lady for his cone.

"Thank you," he said. "You're really a kind person. You fine too, and if I didn't have a girlfriend, I would ask you out on a date."

I reached out to give the man ten dollars. "That's for your sandwich later and thanks for the compliment. Your girlfriend is real lucky to have you. Be sure to tell her that too."

I walked away from the man, not even bothering to look back because I figured his eyes were glued to me, as were the eyes of an Italian man who held the door for me. He was cursed out by his wife for taking a double look.

"What, you gon' break your fucking neck or trip over something for gawking at that bitch? If so, let her pay your muthafucking bills. Let her cook for your ass and leave me the hell alone."

The man didn't have much to say. I kept it moving in my strappy sandals and with my sunglasses shielding my eyes. I was on the inside of the market for a measly ten minutes when I saw someone who looked very familiar to me. I had hoped that it wasn't him, but the closer I got, my thought was correct. It was Malik with his girlfriend. The only reason I assumed she was his girlfriend was due to his arm hanging over her shoulder and the two of them browsing the market while walking side by side. I attempted to move in another direction, but since Malik had picked up his pace, I suspected that he had already seen me. He had the nerve to call out my name, as if we had something to talk about. I wasn't about to be fake with him, so as he headed my way with his dreads in a ponytail, along with a bright smile on his face, my expression remained flat.

"I thought that was you," he said with alcohol on his breath. He removed his arm from around his pint-sized, green-eyed, black chick with thick braids that hung several inches past her shoulders. I wasn't going to confirm if she was cute or not—I really didn't care. My eyes were fixed on him as he attempted to reach out and hug me. I backed away.

"None of that, please. We don't go there anymore, but since we happened to run into each other, why haven't you called to see about your daughter? Why haven't you made any attempts to help me take care of her? How dare you reach out to me for a hug, as if you and I don't have a child that you took it upon yourself to abandon?"

With an embarrassed look on his face, he stepped back to scratch his beard. "I haven't abandoned anybody. You were the one who told me never to call you again. The last time I checked, you did sign those divorce papers, didn't you?"

He was the one person who could really get underneath my skin. I hated to be this way, but I had to let him know that everything between us wasn't as good as he thought it was.

"I surely did sign them, but what does that have to do with our daughter? What does that have to do with you paying child support? Answer that for me, because I would really like to know, Malik."

"You said you didn't want child support, remember? My money was dirty, and you told me to shove it up my ass. So, your child support funds are in my ass. There's a bunch of it in there too, so when you're ready to come get it, just reach for it."

I wanted to punch him in his face. Malik was like an enemy to me. I hated him with a passion. Seeing him made my flesh crawl, and before I did anything stupid, I just turned to walk away from him.

"Nice seeing you," he shouted. "And tell our daughter to call me. I've been waiting for her to break away from you and call me."

I tried, but I just couldn't walk away from that kind of noise. What in the hell did he mean by he was waiting for her to break away from me and call him? I rushed up to ask him about his snide remark that had me fuming.

"Excuse me, fool, but Kendal will never break away from me and call you for anything. You are a low-life idiot, Malik, and you really need to get your reckless life together before it's too late. I'm so thankful that I got rid of you. Kendal's and my life has been—"

"Has been in shambles since I left. I know all about her suspensions from school. Know all about how you've been treating her, and she even told me about that creep you've been with. Good luck with him, and good luck with trying to raise our daughter all by yourself. From what I hear, you're a shitty mother who don't know how to listen. That don't surprise me because you were a shitty wife."

Malik laughed and had the audacity to grab his trick by the waist and walk away from me. My eyes searched my surroundings. I was looking for anything to go bust his damn head wide open. The only thing that snapped me out of my trance was the homeless man I had seen earlier. He put a clear box with a chocolate-coated strawberry in it in front of my face.

"This is for the beautiful lady," he said. "I bought it for my girlfriend, but I changed my mind. I wanted to give it to you."

"No, thanks," I said with a tight face. "Give it to your girlfriend. I'm sure she'll enjoy it."

I was so mad that I didn't even thank the man. I stormed back to my car, and after I got inside, I looked at my phone to see if Brent had called. He hadn't. That pissed me off even more, and knowing that Kendal had said something to Malik had sent me over the edge. She hadn't said a word about that to me. I couldn't wait to find out from her why she hadn't told me and exactly what she'd said to him about me. The thoughts of it all made me sick. I hammered the horn with the palm of my hand, reflecting back to the good life I'd had, before Malik caused it all to fall apart. My mother and stepfather raised me right.

They taught me good morals and values, and all I ever wanted was to marry a man who would be half as good as my stepfather was. I remembered all the love they showed me as a child, and throughout my entire childhood, I didn't want for much. Then, Malik came along with his foolishness. He'd made a mess of my life. I sat thinking about a time when his drug-selling bullshit almost got all of us killed. I had already told him the marriage was done, but it wasn't as if it ended right away.

Kendal and I sat at the kitchen table, putting a puzzle together that had over 1,000 pieces. It was something we had been working on together, just to keep ourselves busy and try to do something fun as mother and daughter. I felt good about spending time with her, especially since Malik and I had been arguing all the time over his new occupation. Kendal had been in a very unstable environment, and I was delighted that Malik would soon be moving out and the divorce papers would be signed. She felt some kind of way about her father not being around anymore, but as we talked about it, she knew it was the right thing to do. She also knew that Malik was the one who had messed up our happy home, and no words could describe how disappointed I was in his failures to stand up and be a real man who took care of his family.

"Mom, what are you doing?" Kendal asked as she noticed my attention divert elsewhere. I was in deep thought about my failed marriage to Malik that I hadn't been helping her with the puzzle. I snapped out of my trance and smiled.

"Forgive me," I said. *"I was just thinking about something that happened earlier."*

We continued to put together the puzzle, and five minutes later, Malik came busting through the door as if someone was chasing him. I wasn't sure what the hell was going on, but I noticed a large plastic bag in his hand that he had tucked underneath his shirt to hide. I got up from the table, following him into our bedroom at the end of a narrow hallway. He tried to be slick by tucking the bag underneath our mattress so I wouldn't see it.

"What are you hiding?" I asked with my hand on my hip. A scarf was tied around my head, and the silk pajama top I wore was at knee level.

"I'm not hiding anything," he said, pacing the room and wringing his hands together. *"Why don't you go back in the kitchen with Kendal? She's calling you, isn't she?"*

I folded my arms across my chest. Malik didn't think I was that stupid, did he? In no way was Kendal calling for me. She probably had her hands shielding her ears so she wouldn't have to listen to what was about to go down.

"First of all, I told you never to bring any of your drugs in this house, but obviously you refuse to listen to me. I also told you that if this is what you choose to do, that was fine. Just know that when you go down, Kendal and I aren't going down with you. Lastly, I really wish you would hurry up and find you somewhere else to stay until the divorce is done. I don't want to subject myself or our daughter to your mess, and you need to get whatever it is underneath that mattress right now, and get it the hell out of here."

Malik waved me off, as if my words didn't mean a thing. "Calm down and stop speaking to me as if you're my mother." He walked over to the window and slightly moved the curtain aside. He peeked outside, as if he was looking for someone. I guess he didn't see anyone because he turned his attention back to me. "Now, as I said before, I don't know what you're talking about. I didn't put anything underneath the mattress—you must be seeing things."

To prove my point, I marched farther into the room and attempted to lift the mattress. Malik shoved me away, causing me to stumble backward. That made me charge at him full force. But he stopped me, again, when he raised his fist and dared me to get in his way. Malik had never put his hands on me before, but his threats angered me more. I challenged him, and before I knew it, we started to tussle. He twisted my arms behind my back, and I kicked his legs while yelling and screaming for him to release me. That's when he did. But he pushed me back on the bed and rushed into another room to go get something that he claimed would silence me.

After he left the room, I hopped off the bed and lifted the mattress. Sure enough, there it was. A healthy bag of marijuana that had to be worth a couple thousand dollars. I snatched it from underneath the bed, and just as I started to rip the package, Malik rushed back into the room. This time, a gun was in his hand. He aimed it at me, and with a devious look in his eyes, he demanded that I put the bag on the bed.

"Do it, Abby, or else I'll shoot! I don't give a damn that you're still my wife, I will blow your damn head off if you don't put that down!"

I stood in total disbelief. The man I had been with for all these years was now threatening to kill me over some fucking dope? Was he serious? This wasn't how it was supposed to be, and as tears streamed down my face, all I could do was tell Malik how much I hated him.

"You're disgusting," I shouted. "I guess you're okay with shooting me, right in front of your own daughter! What kind of man are you, Malik? What has gotten into you, and what did I ever do to you to deserve this?"

Malik turned around, seeing that Kendal was indeed in the doorway. She was crying her heart out too, but she didn't say a word to Malik. He, however, tried to turn all of this on me, as if it was my fault that he decided to become a drug dealer.

"Listen, baby girl," he said, shifting his head from me to her, "you don't know what kind of woman your mama really is. All she did was complain about bills, and now that I'm trying to make a decent living for us, she's still complaining. It is my responsibility to take care of you. I want to have the means to buy you anything you want. Like that coat you showed me the other day. I want you to have that coat, and when Christmas rolls around, you will have it. Don't listen to your mother when she tells you I'm a bad person. I'm not, and your daddy will always take care of you, okay?"

Malik had fed Kendal a bunch of bullshit. I hoped she wasn't falling for it, but when she nodded her head, I wasn't so sure.

"Kendal, go back into the kitchen and finish the puzzle. You don't need to listen to his lies, and trust me when I say I've heard enough."

Kendal listened and walked away from the door. That was when I called Malik's bluff about blowing my brains out and busted the bag of marijuana wide open. Marijuana spilled everywhere, particularly on the carpeted floor and on our sheets. Malik looked at the floor with bugged eyes.

"Shall I get a vacuum for you to clean this up?" I asked.

He dropped the gun on the dresser and ran up to me. "Fucking bitch!" he shouted. "Do you know what I had to do to get that shit? Do you have any idea how much it's worth? I could kill you right fucking now, Abby! What in the hell is wrong with you?"

"It's funny that you asked, as if you don't already know. You're what's wrong with me. I had high hopes for us, Malik, and never did I think there would come a time when I classified you as a poor excuse for a man. I'm sorry about your little weed, but the next time you want to bring that shit here, you'd better well think again."

Just as I got ready to leave the room, I heard hard knocks on the front door. I turned to Malik, who instantly panicked.

"Get . . . Go get Kendal and go hide in a closet. Any closet and don't come out until I tell you to."

"Who is that at the door?" I questioned. "The police? If it is, good. Let me go open the door, so they can come in here and arrest you."

Malik rushed up to me, grabbing my arm. "Hell no, that's not the police! Do what I fucking told you, bitch, and stop all this foolish talk about having me arrested. If you don't listen to me, yo' ass is going to be dead!"

Now fearing for my life, and after listening to several more bangs on the door, I hurried out of the room to go get Kendal. She was already standing in a corner, shivering and afraid of the person cussing through the door.

"Malik, I know you got my shit!" the man shouted. "Open the fucking door, or I'm gon' kick this muthafucka down, come inside, and beat yo' ass!"

His words were enough to have Kendal and me running to a closet. I wanted to call 911, but the cordless phone was somewhere in my room. Malik thought the shit was funny. He laughed at the man, telling him that if he entered our home without permission, there would be a bullet waiting for him on the other side.

"Don't tempt me," Malik said. "You'd better leave now or leave in a goddamn body bag!"

There was a long silence before we heard a crashing sound that traveled all through our quivering bodies. I held Kendal tight; she held me tighter. We could hear Malik and the man arguing over whose dope it really was.

"I can't believe you took my shit!" the man yelled. "I want it back right now, or else you need to up my fucking money!"

"I don't have your dope, and I suggest you go talk to that nigga Lendon who talked about robbing yo' ass just last week! You are barking up the wrong tree. I don't steal from Negroes who don't have nothing that I want. But before you exit, you will have to drop some paper on the table to fix my door!"

"Fuck you and that door. I'm going to go see what's up with Lendon, and if the evidence leads me back here, I'm coming for you, Malik. You can be sure that I'm coming for you."

Malik didn't reply. He was all talk and no action. I wanted to tell that man where he could find his dope, but for now, all I wanted was out of here. As soon as I heard the man speed away, Kendal and I rushed out of the closet. I didn't have time to argue with Malik, and before that man came back, we were out of here.

"Grab your suitcase," I said to Kendal. "And pile it high with everything you want to take with you. We're not coming back here again, so please don't forget a thing!"

Kendal went to her room, I went back to mine. I grabbed two suitcases from the closet, tossing them on the bed. Malik looked at me as if I was the one who had lost my mind.

"Are you going to help me get this shit off the floor or not?" he asked, referring to the marijuana.

I couldn't help but to laugh as I started throwing some of my clothes into the suitcase. "You really shouldn't get high off your own supply, Malik. Obviously, that's what you've been doing because you have totally lost your mind."

He continued to rant as I piled my suitcases so high, I was almost unable to close them. I snatched them off the bed, and as Kendal awaited me in the hallway, I didn't bother to say good-bye or good riddance to Malik. I never wanted to see his face again, and it wouldn't bother me one bit if I didn't. I was not only disgusted with him, but also livid with myself for falling in love with a man like him. My parents taught me better than this; therefore, I knew I deserved better. I guess we all make mistakes, sometimes, when it came to relationships, but I'd be damned if I ever allowed another foolish man like Malik to enter my life again.

Those were my thoughts as I left home that day. After Malik and I were divorced, I got the house, threw out everything that belonged to him, including memories that were oftentimes bad. I knew Kendal was a little upset with me about my immediate action, but she just didn't know what a letdown Malik had truly been to me.

Kendal didn't arrive home until nine thirty that night. I was waiting for her in her bedroom, while sitting on her bed. Her yearbook album was on my lap—I had been paging through it, looking at her photos that resembled me.

"I apologize for being late," she said, tossing a duffle bag on the bed. "Tammi's car stopped working, so I had to wait until her mother got home."

"If that was the case, why didn't you just call me to say that? I could have driven to Tammi's house and picked you up."

"I didn't know if you would be here. You're always with Brent on the weekends, so I thought you had plans."

"I'm not always with Brent, and regardless, you should have called to let me know something. If you didn't want to call me, you could have sent a text message, or you could have reached out to your father like you've been doing."

Kendal didn't respond. She walked over to her closet, sliding it aside. She removed a long shirt and her house shoes.

"Why didn't you tell me you've been speaking to your father? And has he given you any money?"

"I don't care to talk about that right now. I just want to take a shower and get me some sleep because we stayed up all night watching TV."

"You don't get to decide what's up for discussion around here. I asked you a question, and I want some answers."

She released a deep sigh and started to remove her tennis shoes. "Mama, I said I don't want to talk about it. Every time we talk about him, you always start fussing and saying things that I really don't want to hear. I'm tired. All I want to do is get some rest."

I laid her yearbook on the bed, then stood with my arms crossed. "You go ahead and get your rest, but in the morning, we *will* talk about what Malik told me today. I saw him at Soulard. He made it clear that the two of you have been talking. Talking bad about me, and just so you know, I don't appreciate you telling him about things that go on here. It's none of his business."

Kendal shrugged as if none of this mattered. It did to me, because I thought she hadn't spoken to him since our divorce. And if she had spoken to him, why wouldn't she tell me?

"He loves to get you all worked up, and when does it stop, Mama? Our conversations have been brief, only because he's the one who talks negative, not me."

I wanted to push, but I was so on edge right now that I knew the timing wasn't good. I needed to clear my mind and deal with this in the morning.

I tossed and turned all night. Couldn't sleep for nothing because my mind was on Brent. He hadn't called me all day. I reached out to him twice, but my phone calls weren't returned. He had never done anything like this before. I wondered what in the hell was going on, especially when I got a lame-ass excuse from him the following day about how "busy" he'd been.

"I was in meetings all day. Barely had time to grab something to eat. By the time I got back to my hotel room, I was exhausted. I hope you're not upset with me."

I was, but he didn't have to know it. "Why would I be upset with you? If your meetings ran over, so be it."

"You sound a little upset. I can hear it in your voice."

"I'm just concerned about a few things with Kendal, that's all. It has nothing to do with you."

"Anything I can do to help?"

"Nope. Just hurry home. I miss you, and Thursday can't get here soon enough."

"Friday," he said, correcting me. "I won't be back until Friday evening. Hopefully, we can have dinner. I'll let you know for sure."

It was a good thing that he couldn't see me roll my eyes. "Friday sounds good. Let me go ahead and finish my breakfast. I'll try to call you later, okay?"

"Okay, sweetheart. Tell Kendal I said hello, and I hope everything works out between the two of you."

"It will. Thanks."

My tone was dry, and Brent could sense it. I was trying so hard to believe the things he'd said, but for the first time in our relationship, I had bad vibes. Maybe things would get better when he returned. I surely hoped so. In the meantime, I suspected that this would be one of the longest weeks of my life.

Chapter Three

The week had gone by too slowly. Brent and I talked two or three times, that was it. As for my conversation with Kendal, it was brief as well. All she said was that she had spoken to Malik twice. According to her, there was nothing else that needed to be said. I attempted to avoid any arguments with her, simply because I was already hot about Brent. He'd given me the cold shoulder. I didn't like it one bit. He was supposed to return this evening, but he called me this morning to say he was back in town already.

"See, I came home early, just to see you. I hope we're still on for dinner this evening, because I have something very important that I need to speak to you about."

I was at my desk with the phone pushed up to my ear. "If it's that important, why don't you come to the store? I'll leave, and we can do lunch around one or two."

"No, I'd rather wait until later. My work has gotten a little behind. I'm on my way to school to pick up some students' papers I should have graded before I left."

"Okay. Go ahead and handle your business. I'll see you around seven or eight tonight."

"Eight would be great. I miss you, and I can't wait to see you."

The enthusiasm in Brent's voice just wasn't there, but that could have been because he sensed my attitude. It had been there since his first phone call, but I was sure that we would clear the air tonight and move on.

I decided to take my lunch break around noon. Bread Company was always packed around that time, but I was in the mood for a chicken Panini and soup. I drove to the restaurant, but when I saw the long line stretching outside of the door, I changed my mind. I drove down Brentwood Blvd., looking for something else to eat. Nearly every place seemed crowded, but just as I got ready to park my car and go into Chipotle, I saw Brent parking his car on the other side of the parking lot. I didn't want him to see me, so I ducked in my seat, shielding my eyes with glasses. Brent was on his cell phone as he walked across the parking lot, not really paying attention to his surroundings. I wasn't sure where he was headed—possibly, to get something to eat like I was. There was also a chance that he was meeting someone. I chilled for a moment to see if another person showed up, especially since he halted his steps in front of the strip mall. He was still on the phone, but he appeared to be looking around for someone. I was nervous as ever, and if a female showed up, I wasn't sure what I would do. But minutes later, Brent ended his call. He tucked the phone in his pocket, then walked several stores down to a jewelry store that had been in business for years. My heart started to race. Why did he go into a jewelry store, especially when he didn't wear much jewelry? I was so curious that I hurried out of the car but was careful not to be seen. I lowered my head as I walked by the huge windows that provided a clear view of the inside. And in one quick glance, I saw Brent standing at the counter, talking to a woman behind it. I moved all the way to the last windowpane, then stood still. I pretended as if I was looking for someone in the parking lot, but on occasion, I turned my head to glance inside of the store. Brent stood in front of a case that had wedding rings inside of it. The woman was all smiles. She kept nodding her head at him. The only person that ring could have been for was me. Brent was making plans to propose. That's why he wanted me to come over tonight. I was so ecstatic that I wanted to cry. I wanted to rush inside and tell him yes yes yes! I couldn't believe this was happening, and even though I had probably ruined the surprise, I was still shocked, more so happy, to be Mrs. Brent Carson.

Just so he wouldn't see me, I rushed back to my car, deciding to skip lunch altogether. Instead, I went to the gym to work out. It helped me calm myself down. I was so mad at myself for ever doubting Brent. It was a good thing that I didn't tell him how upset I was about not speaking to him while he was away. That would have probably blown everything up in smoke. Silence was golden—sometimes. In this case, it surely was.

I was so hyped that I didn't want to stay at work. When I returned, I told the assistant manager that I wasn't feeling well and needed to go home. I was already off for the entire weekend. I assumed Brent and I would be celebrating our new proposal. We would have the best time ever as a married couple, but the first thing I needed to do was sit down with Kendal and tell her what was about to happen. This would certainly affect her life, and the way she'd felt about Brent had to change.

Kendal had a half day at school, so she was there when I got home. I walked into the kitchen, where she was sitting at the table eating and watching TV. She looked at me as if she was surprised to see me.

"What are you doing home so early? I thought you weren't getting off until six?"

"I was supposed to work late, but something came up. Something I need to talk to you about because it's very important."

"From the look on your face, I can tell that it is. Are you worried about something?"

"No, I'm not worried about anything. Actually, I'm real happy. Something happened earlier, and I think Brent may propose to me tonight. I'm not completely sure, but I have a deep feeling that he's going to ask me to be his wife. How do you feel about that?"

Kendal shrugged and looked out the window as she spoke. "I don't care what y'all do. I guess it doesn't matter that I don't like him, but whatever. As long as you're happy, it is what it is."

Just as I was about to take a seat to discuss this more with Kendal, the doorbell rang. She rushed to it. I followed right after her.

"Are you expecting someone?" I asked. "You know you're not supposed to have company if I'm not here."

Kendal appeared nervous. And when she opened the door, I certainly knew why. There was a young man standing on my porch with a basketball tucked underneath his arm. He looked past Kendal and directly at me.

"I . . . I thought you may want to come outside and play basketball," he said, then shifted his eyes to Kendal.

"No, not right now," she said. "Maybe later."

"Not now, not later," I said, knowing darn well that he wasn't here to play basketball. "How old are you, and how do you know Kendal?"

She turned to me. "Mama, please. You don't—"

"Close your mouth and move out of the way. I asked him a question, and I want some answers."

"We go to school together. I'm seventeen."

"What's your name?"

"Micah."

"Great. Micah, Kendal is on punishment. She can't have any company, especially when I'm not here. So, good-bye."

He walked away, and I shut the door. Kendal marched back into the kitchen with an attitude. "You didn't have to be so mean to him. All he wanted to do was play basketball."

"Basketball, my ass, Kendal. You didn't know I was coming home early, so you invited him over here. I wasn't born yesterday. In case you forgot, I used to be a teenager before too."

"I didn't invite him over here, and what's this about me being on punishment? On punishment for what?"

"On punishment because I felt like saying that to him. And if you keep up with this attitude of yours, you *will* be on punishment."

Kendal pouted and kept her eyes on the TV, ignoring me. Yet again, I didn't feel as if this was the right time to talk to her about my plans with Brent. She and I would probably get into a heated argument. I didn't want anyone, not even her, to ruin this day for me.

"I'm meeting Brent for dinner this evening. Are you planning on doing anything, other than watching TV and being on that computer?"

"Nope. It's all you allow me to do, so the TV it is."

"Kendal, stop talking nonsense. You were just at Tammi's house for the whole weekend. And then when I told you to be home by six, you disobeyed me."

"I told you why I was late. But just like everything else, you never believe me."

I wasn't in the mood to listen to her point the finger at me for every little thing. I tried my best to let her do some of the things she wanted, but the truth is, she had been lying to me about a lot of things. But instead of calling her out on those things, I headed to my room and removed my work clothes. I took a hot, soothing bath, and then chilled for a few hours, reading a book. Brent called, just as I was finishing up the last chapter.

"Hello, sweetheart," he said, seeming more upbeat. "I'm all done for the day, so whenever you're ready, you can head my way. We're staying in again. I ordered Chinese. It should be here within an hour or so."

"Chinese sounds good. I'll be there soon, okay?"

"Hurry. I miss you."

He didn't have to tell me twice. I had my sexy black jumper all ready to go, and with a plunging neckline, sexy was written all over it. The pants were wide-legged, and the high heels I wore made me taller than what I already was. My attire was a bit much for just going to his house, but this was, no doubt, a special occasion. I wiggled my fingers in front of my eyes, wondering what kind of ring would suit my finger. I didn't care if it was a one carat diamond or ten. Whatever Brent gave me, I would be completely satisfied. Our wedding day was also on my mind. I wasn't sure what day he would choose, but figuring that it would be left up to me, I decided any time in the summer would be fine.

Kendal was in her bedroom, sitting in front of the computer. I heard her speaking to someone over the phone, and when she laughed and called Micah by his name, I cleared my throat. She quickly turned her head.

"I'm leaving," I said. "I shouldn't be long, but if you need me, call my cell phone."

She waved her fingers in the air and continued to talk to Micah. I left the house, very concerned about where my relationship with my daughter was headed. She would be sixteen years old soon. I had a feeling that things between us weren't going to improve. I planned to talk to Brent about any suggestions he had to help improve my relationship with Kendal. He was good with kids. I would take his advice and run with it.

Several minutes later, I arrived at Brent's place. This time, he opened the door with a bottle of wine in his hand. He was casually dressed in a pair of jeans and a dark blue V-neck T-shirt that showed his chest. There was a diamond-stud earring in his ear. I had only seen him wear it a few times before. His bald head had a shine, and his trimmed goatee made my heart melt. My future husband sure as heck was handsome.

"You look amazing," he said, widening the door for me to come inside. "I feel like a bum. You didn't have to get so dressed up to come here."

"True, but you already know how I am. This jumped out at me in my closet, so I decided to put it on."

Brent couldn't wait to grab me in his arms. His arms were locked around my waist, lips were already pressed against mine.

"Sweet," he said. "I surely missed those lips, but not as much as I missed this."

Brent caught me off guard when he lifted me off my feet, carrying me into his bedroom. He sat me on the bed, then squatted to remove my shoes.

"I hope you don't mind that I asked the Chinese delivery driver to leave our food on the porch. There are other things I want to tend to right now, if you'll let me."

No argument from me whatsoever. Brent pulled his shirt over his head, and after he unzipped the back of my jumper, he lay over me. We started to kiss and grind against each other. I eased my hands in the inside of his jeans to massage his ass. I loved the way it felt when it tightened. I also loved how his meat felt inside of me. I was in a rush to proceed to the next level—so was he.

"I wish that we could do this forever," he said between kisses. My jumper had hit the floor, and without a stich of underclothes on, I opened my legs wide, inviting Brent inside.

"We can go on like this forever," I said. "And we will."

Brent tapped his steel against my slit, before navigating it inside of me. I locked my lips on him, and as he thrusted in and out of me, I was in another world. For some reason, sex between us felt better than it had ever felt before. He wasn't as gentle as he had always been, and I could tell from the mild roughness he added that he had missed me. He grinded harder. Kissed me as if my lips were the last thing on earth. Touched me all over and sucked my breasts like they were juicy melons. His pace was at a speed that brought forth sweat beads on his forehead. And with my legs thrown high over his shoulders, he pounded away to bring down my juices.

"I don't ever want to be without this wet pussy," he moaned. "You make me feel so good, baby. Damn, this is good."

Making it even better, I turned on my stomach, exposing my pretty ass to him. He loved to work me from behind, but it wasn't long before his steel sprayed my insides with semen.

"I . . . I need more." He was barely able to catch his breath. "Give me a minute, and then I'm going to milk you dry."

"Never, but it will be my pleasure to get you ready for the second round."

Brent rolled over, and I lay on top of him. I pecked his chest, swiped my tongue across his nipples, and then lowered myself to make his limp muscle rise to the occasion again. Within a few minutes, his steel stretched my mouth. His head rubbed against my throat. The deeper it went, the more his steel expanded.

"Mmmmm, there you go, baby. Get it all in there. All of it."

I was successful at doing just that. And as the taste of his dick got even better, I started to rain on the other end. His fingers were doing quite a number on me—I could barely keep still.

"The sound of that is like music to my ears," he said. "Let's shoot for the stars together."

Brent's fingers moved like a piano player inside of me, and as my head bobbed up and down from excitement, we finally came together. I had never been more pleased with his performance. While we lay next to each other in bed, I told him just that.

"I mean, you're always good, but I felt as if you really put your foot in it tonight. What's so special about tonight?" I teased. "Maybe you should take more vacations in the future."

He laughed while cuddling me in his arms. "Maybe I will, but a week is too much. You are special, and there is no question that I'm real excited about you."

I smiled, wondering if this was the moment he would break the good news. I snuggled against his chest, and as his fingertips lightly rubbed my ass, I closed my eyes.

"I'm so happy about our relationship, Brent. Never, ever did I think I would find a man like you. I truly thought men like you didn't exist. I'm so lucky to have you in my life."

He remained silent. I opened my eyes, and when I looked up at him, he leaned in for a quick kiss.

"Thanks for saying that," he said. "We both are lucky, and I've been happy about our relationship too. But there always comes a time when things have to change. Things that are beyond our control, and we wish they could be different."

My stomach tightened. I was about to pee on myself, I was so excited. Change was coming to us real soon, and I could only imagine what our future would look like. I wasn't sure if I would move into Brent's house with him or if he planned to move in with me. Then again, looking for a new house with him would be fun.

I rubbed my fingers against his chest. "I wish things could be different between us too. I love our relationship, but there comes a time when we will have to consider taking it to the next level."

He didn't reply, but I felt movement in his body. I thought he was getting ready to get up and get the ring.

"But I don't know if we're ready for that step," I continued. "You tell me. Are you ready to move to the next level with me or not?"

Brent released a deep sigh. He kissed my forehead before sitting up in bed. His move caused me to lift my head from his chest and sit up too. And when he reached for my hands, he held them with his. His eyes were locked with mine.

"If there is any woman I would consider moving to the next level with, that woman would be you. But, unfortunately," he cleared his throat and swallowed, "I can't go to that next level with anyone right now. There are a lot of things going on in my life, and even though I'm confused about a few things, I do know what I want."

Confused? Hell, I was too, especially by what he'd just said. A frown was on my face. My eyes narrowed as I looked at him.

"What's unfortunate, and why can't you go to the next level? If you know what you want, I assume that you want me."

He nodded. "I do, but it's not that simple anymore. What I'm saying is—" He paused to look away. A tiny knot in my stomach started to form.

I lifted my hand to his face, turning it so he could look at me again.

"What are you saying? You're not making much sense here. If you have something to say, please say it."

He swallowed hard while staring into my eyes. "What I'm saying is, this relationship has been amazing, and I like you a lot. But the truth is, I'm still in love my wife. I never stopped loving her, and this has been so hard for me."

I released a deep breath and smiled. "Brent, stop kidding around. This is not the time to be joking around. You won't get any laughs from me, talking like that."

Brent's expression remained serious. "I'm sorry, baby, but this is not a joke. I wish I didn't have to say this to you, but I could never find the right moment to tell you that my wife and I had been discussing reconciliation. She finally agreed to give our marriage another chance. She's going to move back to St. Louis in a few weeks, and I told her that my relationship with you would end."

I stared at Brent without a blink. My breathing was no more. The knot in my stomach was so tight that it hurt. Tears welled in my eyes. I was speechless. I waited for him to say he was just kidding, but those words never came. I wanted him to tell me I could breathe again . . . to relax, but that didn't happen. All he said again was, "I'm sorry. So sorry and forgive me for not telling you this sooner."

My mouth opened, but I was unable to speak. I finally blinked, bringing down a slow tear that ran over my cheek. Brent reached out to hold me, and as I sat like a zombie, he rocked me in his arms.

"Please don't cry. This hurts me too. You are such a wonderful woman, but I had to choose. I didn't want to string you along, and continuing to be unfaithful to my wife isn't something I want to do."

Every time he said "his wife," I flinched. A painful jab punched me in the gut and my mind started racing. I was completely caught off guard. None of this made sense, not one single thing.

"I understand if you're upset. But please don't be mad. We had something real special, and I don't ever want you to forget how much you meant to me."

The truth was I could only take so much of this. The pain was unbearable. It was worse than anything I'd felt before, simply because I had made Brent out to be something that he truly wasn't. I pulled myself away from him, just to look into his eyes. I wanted him to look deep into my hurt, even though I was sure that it didn't matter. The next thing I did was lift my hand and slap the shit out of him. His head jerked to the side, and that's when my fist crashed into the side of his face. He jumped off the bed, not knowing what was coming next as he held the side of his face, displaying a frown.

"Damn it, Abby, what in the hell did you do that for? Shit!"

I spoke through gritted teeth. "Tell me right now that this is a fucking joke! Tell me that you are not married, and you have not allowed me to fall in love with a goddamn married man!"

Brent rubbed his forehead and squeezed his eyes together. He started to pace the floor with his eyes focused on me. "I didn't know you were in love with me. Since when? You never said that shit, and I never said I loved you either."

Boom! Yet again, I was stunned. My mouth was wide. I felt my blood about to boil over. "Hell no, you never said it, but you didn't have to! You said a whole lot of other shit, and wha . . . What about the ring you purchased today? I guess that was for her, not me, right?"

"How did you know what I purchased today? Have you been following me?"

He was starting to sound real stupid. I was so frustrated that I hopped off the bed, just to get closer to him. And as I stood within inches of him, he could barely look at me.

I pointed at his temple, pushing it with my finger. "You know what? Fuck you and fuck your ring. To hell with your wife, 'cause she has got to be some kind of fool to be with a man like you. I mean, how could you, Brent? How can you stand there and do this to me? No warning, no anything. Just—just fuck my brains out, and then tell me to go to hell! That's cold. You're one cruel motherfucker, and I have never met anyone as cold as you."

Tears streamed down my face as I snatched my jumper off the floor. Brent watched as I got dressed, not saying a word to me. I swear if I had a gun, I would have used it. There was so much more that I wanted to say and do to him. I was fighting to maintain the little composure I'd had.

"No matter what you think of me," he said softly, "I did care about—"

"Shut the hell up talking to me!" I screamed. My voice was so loud that it caused him to cock his head back and gaze at me in shock. "Don't you dare stand there and talk about how much you cared about me! You're a fucking liar! All you ever wanted from me was some ass until you were able to patch things up with your wife!"

I looked up, shaking my head and thinking again about *his wife*. Did she even exist, and where in the hell had she been for over a year? At this point, it really didn't matter. I was getting the hell out of there, and Brent would never have to worry about seeing me again. I snatched my shoes from the floor, and then I rushed by him so I could leave. He followed, still trying to apologize and clear up the severe damage he'd done.

"I wish you wouldn't leave like this. Our relationship was more than sex and you know—"

I swung around, putting my finger near his face again. The devilish glare in my eyes warned him to back the hell up. He did.

"What am I supposed to do, huh? Stay here and throw a fucking party with you to celebrate your wife's return? Get the hell away from me, Brent. If you want to live to see another day, you should not say another word to me."

He took my advice and stayed several feet away from me as well. When I pulled open the door, I saw a brown bag that had our Chinese food in it. The aroma hit me immediately, so I snatched up the bag, hurling it in his direction. The bag busted, causing the rice and gravy to spill all over him. It was the least I could do before charging down the steps and getting into my car.

I watched as Brent slowly closed the door and turned off the porch light. Knowing that this was the end of our relationship, I laid my head on the steering wheel, crying like a baby while holding my aching stomach that delivered an insurmountable amount of pain.

Chapter Four

I was miserable. Miserable as hell more like it, and I thought that after a few weeks had gone by, I would start to feel better. That was in no way the case. I couldn't stop thinking about Brent . . . more specifically, about what he had done. I felt dissed on so many different levels. I couldn't believe he had done this to me. How could he fuck my brains out like that, and then turn around and say he was moving on? I had made myself sick just thinking about it. I kept having flashbacks of that day, thinking about what I should have done to him. I even thought about what I should have said, and needless to say, I let him off easy. Too easy.

Now, he was living happily ever after again with his wife. He thought he could just swat me away like a pesky fly and wash his hands of me. I had been thinking of some devious shit to do to him, and even though those things seemed so out of character for me, there was no question that Brent had to pay for the suffering he had caused me. I hadn't been able to eat much or go to work. Since I had plenty of paid time off, I used that time off work to try to get myself together. That was two weeks ago. I still wasn't quite right yet, and I hadn't a clue what I could do to make myself feel better.

Spending time with Kendal was an option, but she was so negative about my breakup with Brent that I didn't want to be around her. I let her go to Tammi's house as she had asked, and whenever she got out of school, she always mentioned somewhere else she had to be. I wasn't in the mood to get into a confrontation with her, especially since she had the audacity to say to me, *"I told you Brent was no good. Why would you think he wanted to get married? He would never be considered a father of mine."*

Her words cut me to the core. How did my child know that he wasn't worth two cents, yet I thought he was the best thing ever? I couldn't have been that blind; then again, I was. Brent was fake, and the truth is, he used me during his downtime with his wife. There was no other way to simply put it. There was no love between us. He'd made that quite clear. And when all was said and done, he chose her instead of me. His decision would have made sense to me, had I known the bastard was married. Of course, his wife was the priority, but the way he kept her a secret was totally uncalled for. Damn him. And damn her too.

I lay across the bed with a wet towel slapped across my forehead. My head kept hurting, maybe because my thoughts were all over the place. I didn't know what my next move would be, but I surely wanted to know what Brent's wife looked like. He mentioned that she was moving back to St. Louis in a few weeks. I wondered if she was at his house with him. The only way for me to find out was for me to go over there and see for myself. I could just do a quick drive-by to see if things at the Carson household had changed. I remained on the bed for a few minutes, trying to talk myself out of going over there. But the anger inside of me took over. All I wanted to do was see her. Maybe even talk to her, one day, to find out more about her and Brent's marriage. Why did they separate to begin with? Was there someone else involved, and where, exactly, did she move to? Most importantly, why did she decide to reconcile with him? Did she really know about me? So many questions flooded my mind. She had answers. So did Brent, but I didn't want to say anything else to him until the time was right.

I sluggishly walked to the closet to put on some clothes. I hadn't done much to my hair, so I brushed it back, until it lay flat on my head. Makeup was the last thing I wanted on my face, so I didn't bother. I did, however, need something on my dry lips, so I moistened them with Chap Stick. Afterward, I snatched my keys from my nightstand; then I took the forty-five-minute drive to Brent's place.

To my surprise, just as I turned the corner, a gray Kia Sorento was backing out of the driveway. I could see a woman inside, but her face wasn't visible to me yet. All I could tell was her hair was nearly shaved off, and her skin was light. I got a better view of her when her vehicle stopped at the red light, and I pulled my vehicle next to hers. I immediately thought of Amber Rose. The woman in the car had the same cut as she, and her glowing caramel skin was the same. Her lips were covered with a pink gloss and dark sunglasses covered her eyes. I could tell she was fit, simply by looking at the toned muscles in her arms as she held the steering wheel. The second she shifted her head in my direction, I turned my head. We both waited for the light, and when it changed, she sped off. I told myself not to follow her, but I was so anxious to find out if she was Brent's wife. So from a distance, I watched her pull into a gas station to get gas. When she exited the car, I pursed my lips. Jealousy was written all over my face. Her body was almost perfect. The jeans she wore were melted on her healthy curves, and her midriff was flatter than mine. I guess Brent had a thing for sexy women. She was that, and then some.

The woman pumped gas into her car while appearing to examine her surroundings. I hoped she didn't notice my car parked across the street, but when her head shifted toward my direction, I drove off with another car that was beside me. I turned on a dead-end street, and by the time I did a U-turn, she was back on the road. Minutes later, she parked in front of a Laundromat. She lifted her trunk, removing two baskets of clothes. I watched as she carried them inside. Her strut confirmed her confidence. I never expected for the competition to be this steep. Then again, I wasn't competing for Brent anymore. I just wanted some kind of revenge for what he had done to me.

Remembering that I had a small rug in my trunk, I got out of my car to get it. I went into the Laundromat, pretending as if I was there to wash my rug. The woman I assumed was Brent's wife had already started to fill the washing machine. She had a lot of camouflage-printed clothes, along with white T-shirts. I used the machine right next to her, even though there were plenty of machines not in use. There were also five other women in the Laundromat washing clothes. They were talking loud, laughing, and yelling at their kids.

"Boy, didn't I tell you to come over here and sit down?" one woman said with her hand on her hip. "You got two seconds to do what I say or else!"

She was ignored by the child. I saw Brent's wife shake her head, and that's when I spoke up.

"It's a shame, isn't it?" I said with a smile on my face. I stuffed the rug into the washing machine.

"Very much so. And as you can see, she's ignoring him, just as he's ignoring her. I hope he doesn't break one of those machines he keeps kicking."

"Right. And if he does, I would put some money on it that she won't offer to pay for it."

We laughed. She looked at the rug I had stuffed into the washer. "That's kind of big. I'm not sure if you'll get that to come clean in there. You may want to use one of those fifty-pound washers over there."

She pointed to a larger machine against the wall.

"You don't think this one will work?"

She shrugged her shoulders. "Your rug will fit, but I doubt that it'll come clean."

I nodded and took her advice. "Maybe I should use a bigger one. I was trying to save myself a little change, but I guess you're right."

I removed the rug from the washer, then walked away to put it in another machine. I was still close to Brent's wife, and when her cell phone rang, I was able to eavesdrop on her conversation.

"I just got here, babe. I don't know how long I'm going to be, but if you want to come join me you can." She paused and laughed at the caller's reply. "Okay. See you soon. Love you too, honey."

I assumed that had to be Brent. If he was going to join her, that would be interesting. I wasn't sure if I would hang around or not, but I certainly wasn't going anywhere until my rug was finished.

I coughed, then made my way back over to her, pretending as if I didn't have enough change for the washer.

"I hate to stick my dollars in that change machine back there, because it always takes my money. You wouldn't happen to have change for two dollars, would you?"

At first, she didn't say anything. Just gazed into my eyes, before blinking. "I might have some change." She dug into her pocket, pulling out several quarters and a few dimes. "Sorry, but this is all I have. There's a convenience store next door. They may be able to give you change over there."

Something in her eyes told me she knew who I was. I wasn't so sure yet, so I kept the conversation going.

"I'll go see if they will. And thanks for checking . . . Uh, what's your name?"

Without hesitating, she extended her hand to mine. "Lajuanna. And no problem. Sorry I didn't have it."

My brows furrowed as I pulled my hand away from hers. "Lajuanna? You look so familiar. Your name rings a bell. What school did you go to?"

"I got my degree from Webster University. As for high school, I went to Parkway Central."

"I didn't go to either of those schools, but I'm thinking that I know you from work or something. I worked at Express Scripts for four years. Now, I work at Macy's. Maybe I've seen you shopping in there or something."

"I'm not sure. I've been overseas for a while, and I just got back. That doesn't mean I don't love to shop, because I do. All day, every day."

We both laughed again. It was hard to read her, especially when she shot me a hard stare again.

"I'm a shopaholic too," I said. "My husband hates that I work at Macy's. Every time he looks up, I'm coming through the door with bags in my hand."

"I know how that is. My *husband* gets pretty upset when I shop too much too. He often goes with me, just to keep track of what I'm spending."

"Smart man. Very clever man, and, uh, by the way, my name is Angie. Angie Carson."

She pointed at herself. "I'm a Carson too. Sure we're not related?"

We laughed again—this time it came across as being real fake. Hell no, we weren't related, but we damn sure had something in common.

"I think the whole world is related," I said, continuing the small talk. "Names don't mean a thing."

"I agree. And—"

The ringing of her cell phone interrupted us. She looked at it to see who the caller was.

"Excuse me for a minute. This is my sweet *husband* calling me again."

Sweet, my ass, especially not after the way he treated me. She turned her back to talk, but I still heard what she said.

"I thought I put it in the closet. Look in there, babe. If it's not there, I'll find it when I get home." She paused, then continued speaking. "Okay, I will. I'm hungry too, so why don't you meet me here? I should be done, I guess, in about another hour or so." Whatever he said, she replied, "Okay." After that, she hit the end button on her phone.

She looked at me this time, but I pretended to be focused on the TV mounted on the wall. Our conversation didn't continue, and instead, she walked over to a snack machine to get some pretzels. I wasn't sure how I was going to stir up another conversation with her, but I was sure of one thing. She was Brent's wife. The tiny diamond ring on her ring finger was nothing to brag about though. I wondered if it was the one he had picked out the other day, or if it was one she'd had all along. I figured it wouldn't hurt to ask, and as she stepped away from the food machine, I was right there.

"That's a beautiful ring on your finger. Your husband has very good taste."

She lifted her hand, wiggling her fingers as she looked at the ring. "Yes, he does have good taste, especially when he chose me." She paused and waited for a response. I didn't bother to reply, so she kept talking.

"I lost the first ring he gave me," she said. "He just replaced it. I think it's nice too. I've been getting compliments on it all day."

She lied. The ring wasn't all that, and it really wasn't noticeable. I was glad that crap was on her finger and not mine.

"Well, Angie," she said, "let me get back to my clothes. It was nice talking to you."

"Same here. And I bet when I get home, I'm going to remember exactly where I know you from."

"Probably so."

She walked away to tend to her clothes in the washer. I wanted to hang around for a while, just in case Brent showed up, but I decided against it. At this point, I knew who she was, and that was good enough for me. I made my way to the door, but turned when I heard Lajuanna call me Angie.

"You're not forgetting your rug, are you?" she said. "Or are you on your way to the convenience store to get change?"

I had forgotten all about that stupid rug. I didn't really need it, so leaving it wasn't a big deal. "I'll come back to get it later. I have a few quick errands to run."

"Okay, Angie. Or is it Abby? I think it's Abby, and for the record, *you're* the one who looks very familiar to me. Brent told me all about you. So do me a favor now that I'm home for good. Make sure you and I never meet again."

I was a little shocked that she knew who I was, and at first, I didn't even know how to respond. A few seconds later, I replied with a smile on my face.

"Yes, Abby, not Angie. And as for your no-good husband, tell him to go to hell for me. You and I have no reason to meet again, and that's because you don't have anything I want anymore. If that changes, I'll see you around."

My eyes cut that bitch like a sharp knife. I rolled them, hard, before finally pushing on the door to leave. If she thought she would never see me again, she was crazy. From that moment on, I decided to make her and Brent's life a living hell.

On the drive home, my mind was all over the place. I wondered what else Brent had told Lajuanna about us. I also wondered if she had seen me following her. More than anything, would she tell him about our little encounter today? If she did, I was sure he would call me.

As expected, just as I pulled into my driveway, my cell phone rang. It was Brent. I smiled before putting the phone up to my ear.

"I was just thinking about you," I said. "It's been awhile since you called. What a surprise."

"I'm sure you already know the reason for my call. Lajuanna told me about your visit at the Laundromat. I hope you haven't been following her, and if you are, please don't go there. It's time for us to move on. I've made my decision."

I couldn't believe his tone. This wasn't the Brent I had been with for the past year, was it? He needed to rethink how he spoke to me . . . or else.

"I'm perfectly fine with your decision. Your wife just happened to be at the same location as me. I don't know what she told you, but I know what I was there to do. That was to wash my rug."

"I don't believe that for one minute. I have no idea what you're up to or why you think it was a good idea to follow her, but whatever your game plan is, cancel it. The last thing I want to do is get a restraining order against you. If there are any more 'coincidences' like today, I will do what I have to do."

This fool pissed me off. My grip tightened on the phone. It was a good thing that he couldn't see the tight expression on my face.

"A restraining order, Brent? Really? I'm free to go wherever I wish, so chill with that nonsense. You're starting to sound like you're on edge over there. What are you so worried about, especially if you're satisfied with the choice you made?

Sounds to me like you don't want to see me because you're worried about not being able to control yourself."

"I'm not worried about anything. Just stay away from me and my wife. You do that, we're good."

He ended the call, leaving me more determined to seek revenge against him. How dare he speak to me the way he did. Just who did he think he was? I couldn't believe that he didn't suspect there would be some kind of consequences for dumping me the way he did.

I went inside to calm myself down and relax. A glass of wine in my hand, I paced the floor thinking about my next move. The first thing I had to do was find a man who could help me make Brent jealous. I didn't want him to think I was over here lonely and suffering because of what he'd done. I wanted him to think I'd had someone else on the side all along. It wouldn't be easy for me to find a man who would play this game with me. They would definitely want something out of it—maybe even money. Money was cool, especially since I wasn't about to give up the goodies for favors. There had to be someone who would do it for money, but who? I bit into my nail, taking a tiny bite. Then it hit me. He would be perfect. I smiled at my thoughts; the plan in my head was brilliant.

Chapter Five

The following day, I drove to the Soulard Market, hoping that I would see the homeless man again. Behind the rugged beard and dusty, wavy hair, he was a handsome man. His body showed strength. Muscles were visible, and his light brown eyes spoke volumes. The last time I was here, he asked if I'd had any work for him to do. I did. He was about to become the new and improved man in my life. Hopefully, he would approve.

I browsed around for an hour or so, buying fruits, fish, and veggies, while looking for the man. There were a few homeless people walking the streets. I spotted one man lying on a bench. I didn't, however, see the man I was looking for. The man I saw was Jeff the masseur. He rushed up to me, as if we had been longtime best friends.

"Sweet Pea," he screeched as he gave me a tight hug. "I thought you were supposed to call me, girl."

"I intended to, but I've had a lot on my mind since that day. Brent and I are no longer together. I'm not sure if he told you that bit of information or not."

Jeff threw his hand back and poked out his lips. "Chile, that doesn't surprise me one bit. Brent runs through women like I run through men. I honestly didn't think it was that serious between the two of you. More than anything, I thought it was just a fuck thang."

His words stung. Funny how everyone else saw Brent, with the exception of me. I pretended as if I wasn't as hurt as I really was.

"It couldn't have been serious, especially since he's married. I didn't even know he was married until a few weeks ago."

"What?" Jeff shouted and placed his hand on his chest. "Come on, girl, it's me you talking to. How in the hell didn't you know he was married? And I know you didn't think you were the only one."

"Truthfully, I didn't know he was married. He never wore a ring, and he lived alone. I was with him for one whole year. I never saw anything—" I paused when I looked over Jeff's shoulder, seeing exactly who I was looking for. "Jeff, I'm sorry but I have to go. I'll call you soon, okay?"

"Okay, Sweet Pea," he yelled as I hurried away from him to catch up with my new man. He was walking down the street, strolling a buggy with groceries in it.

"Excuse me, sir," I shouted from several feet away. He was walking so fast that I could barely catch up with him. His chocolate skin looked sweaty, and his hanging cargo shorts displayed his muscular calves. There was no question in my mind that after he was cleaned up, he would be perfect.

"Sir, wait!" I shouted again, causing him to turn around. When he saw me, he halted his steps. I was finally able to catch up with him.

"Hi," I said. "I'm sorry to bother you, but I wanted to speak to you about the offer you made me a few weeks ago. Do you remember meeting me?"

He scratched his head. I could hear how dry his scalp was. "Yes, I remember you. You're the lady who gave me some money and bought ice cream for me."

"Yes, that's me. And you asked if I had any work for you to do around my house. I have plenty of work for you. What kind of work do you do?"

"Carpentry, lawn work, cleaning . . . Whatever you need me to do."

"That's great. I have some ideas, but do you think we can go somewhere and talk about what I need you to do? I'll pay you for your time."

The man nodded, then nudged his head down the street. "I was on my way home. If you don't mind following me, we can go to my place. It's less than five minutes away."

I didn't think he would do anything stupid, but just in case, I already had a can of mace in my purse. I walked side by side with him, kicking up a conversation so I could get to know him better.

"My name is Abby. Yours?"

"I'm Clinton. Clinton Jackson."

"Okay, Mr. Jackson, if you don't mind me asking, why are you out of work? I actually thought you were homeless. It's good to know that you aren't."

"No, I'm not homeless. I have a one-bedroom studio apartment that I've been living in for the past two years. I used to work construction, but the company I worked for moved to another city. I thought it would be easy for me to find another job, but I quickly learned that construction jobs don't come easy, especially for a black man like me who was once incarcerated. I was lucky that the company hired me when I got out of jail. But I haven't been so lucky since they left."

"What were you in jail for?"

He paused before answering. "For selling drugs. Got a judge who was eager to make an example out of me. Told me I needed to learn a lesson, even though I didn't have any prior convictions. He gave me fifteen years, and the rest is history."

"I'm sorry to hear that. The system is so against blacks. Hopefully, our next president will do something about this unfair judicial system."

"They're all talk and no action. That includes the president. Nothing will change, and I will put every dime that you pay me on it."

I felt like him, so I didn't bother making that bet. We continued to talk about the unfair judicial system, and when we reached the apartment building he lived in, I was reluctant to go inside. It wasn't as if it was in a bad neighborhood, but the building looked broken down. The white door that opened to four studio apartments was filthy. When I did enter, the first thing I saw was the wooden stairs that creaked and looked as if they were about to cave in. The carpeted hallway was covered with stains, and the strong smoky smell almost made me want to pass out.

"You have to excuse this place. It's all I can afford right now. My girlfriend is here too, but she may be asleep."

I was surprised to hear that he had a girlfriend, but she wouldn't be no problem for me. He put the key in the door to turn the lock. When we entered his studio apartment, it wasn't as bad as I thought it would be. There wasn't much furniture at all—just a wicker chair with a fake plant next to it. The fireplace had a rug in front of it, and to my right was a tiny kitchen with two folding chairs facing each other. The smell of Pine-Sol was in the air, but the space wasn't 100 percent clean. Dust was caked on the windowsills, and a box of Cornflakes was on the kitchen floor. A dirty rag hung over the sink where dishes were piled pretty high. And the bedroom was sectioned off by a white wrinkled curtain. I saw a mattress on the floor, and when a shadowy figure appeared, I figured it was his girlfriend.

"Velma, come here," he said. "I want you to meet this nice lady who wants me to do some work for her."

Velma came from around the curtain with her long, nappy hair sitting wildly on her head. The pink nightgown she wore had stains on it, and a pedicure and manicure were needed badly. Her brown skin was just as ashy as Clinton's was. I couldn't tell if she was on drugs or not, but her frail frame implied that she was. As she looked me over with her beady eyes, I couldn't help but to think about how Clinton implied he didn't want to cheat on her when I first saw him. If she could keep a man faithful, hell, why couldn't I? I extended my hand to hers.

"Hi, Velma. I met Clinton a few weeks back. I'm here because I would like for him to do some work for me. And, by the way, you have a nice cozy place here."

She didn't bother to shake my hand. "There ain't nothin' cozy or nice about livin' here, so stop lyin'." She looked at Clinton. "I told you it's not a good idea to bring people over here. But since you never listen to what I say, what kind of work does she want you to do?"

"I don't know yet. That's what we came here to holla about."

There was no way for me to tell Clinton what I really wanted him to do for me, so I had to think of something fast.

"I would like for him to build me and my daughter some shelves in our walk-in closets. We have a lot of clothes and shoes that need to be organized."

"Must be nice," she said, slightly rolling her eyes. "Everybody ain't able."

I wanted to tell this heifer with an attitude to get a job and clean this rat-trap up instead of lying around sleeping all day. She obviously didn't like me; jealousy traveled deep in her eyes.

"I would love to work on your closets," Clinton said. "But let me put these groceries in the fridge and find out what Velma wants to eat tonight. After that, we can finish our discussion."

As Clinton and Velma made their way to the kitchen, I walked over to a small bay window with a seat in front of it. That was where I waited until Clinton was finished. I envisioned him dressed in a suit, clean shaven, and sprayed with cologne. He would instantly become an eight on a scale from one to ten. His hair and eyes are what sold me. Brent would also be jealous of Clinton's physique. I couldn't wait to tell him what I really needed him for, but I refused to go into details in front of Velma. She kept sneaking peeks at me and wincing. All I did was smile and turn my head in another direction, as if I was looking at something outside.

"I'm not eating anything until she leaves," Velma said in a whisper, loud enough for me to hear. "So hurry up with your conversation so she can go."

"Calm down, all right? I'm trying to make us some money. You about to blow it with that attitude you got."

I pretended as if I didn't hear their conversation. And when Clinton came up to me, he asked if I would follow him to the hallway outside his door to talk.

"Sure. That's fine with me." I stood and waved to Velma on my way out. "Have a great day. Nice meeting you."

To no surprise, she didn't respond. And as soon as Clinton and I stepped in the hallway, he apologized for her behavior.

"No need to apologize. If I had a man as handsome as you are, I would probably behave the same way."

He blushed—so sexy. "Thanks, but, uh, when do you want me to get started on those closets?"

"How about tomorrow? Tomorrow morning, if you can. I live about forty or so minutes away from here. Will you be able to find a ride or would you like for me to come here and pick you up?"

He lowered his head, looking embarrassed. "I don't have a ride, but I can catch MetroLink to the closest stop near your place."

"You don't have to do that. Just be ready in the morning. Bring whatever you need to measure my closets, and then we'll go to Home Depot to get the materials you'll need. Until then, do you have any idea how much you'll charge me."

"I won't know until I see your closets. It shouldn't be that much, though. I'm just grateful for the work."

"If you do a good job, I may have some other things for you to do. I don't mind paying people who take good care of me."

Just as those words left my mouth, the door swung open. Velma glanced at me before shifting her eyes to Clinton.

"Are you done yet? I'm ready to eat now."

"We're finished," I said, answering for him. "I'll see you in the morning. Thanks again."

"You're welcome."

I walked off, and you had better believe that when I turned around, Velma was evil eyeing me. I sensed that she would be a problem, but as long as she didn't know where I lived or what I intended to do with her man, I was good.

The next morning, I said good-bye to Kendal as she was on her way to school. We seemed to be doing okay lately. My only issue with her was her smart mouth.

"Don't forget that I'm staying after school today," she said. "I'll catch the activity bus home. Will you be here when I get here?"

"I should be. Why? Because you want to invite your little boyfriend over here again?"

"Nope. He won't be invited over here ever again, especially after how you treated him. I hope Brent won't be here either, and it feels so good not to have to see his ugly face again."

Kendal was looking for an argument, but I tried my best to ignore her. I locked the door after she left and glared at her through the window as she walked to the bus stop. Little did she know, her little attitude and comments about Brent were starting to work me. If she thought she was going to come between us, she was sadly mistaken. Some kids were out of line, especially the spoiled-ass ones who'd been given everything on a silver platter. I winced and stepped away from the window to go put on some clothes. Minutes later, I headed to Clinton's place to pick him up.

On the drive there, I made a detour to see if there was anything interesting happening at Brent's place. His car was gone, but his wife's car was still there. I parked my car next to the curb, and before I got out, I removed a pocketknife from my glove compartment. The knife had a sharp blade on it and a pointed edge. I felt a need to get her back for telling Brent that I followed her to the Laundromat. In addition to that, I didn't appreciate her threatening me. This was my answer to her threat.

I made my way up the driveway, bending down so no one would see me. I stabbed her back left tire, and in an instant, I could hear air seeping from it. I casually walked back to my car, but to my surprise, a nosy-ass white man driving by saw me. He lowered his window, calling out to me.

"Hey, hey!" he shouted as he slowly drove beside me. "Did you just poke that tire with a knife?"

I halted my steps and looked at him. "As a matter of fact, I just did. And I'm in the mood to poke something else, so you may want to drive off and mind your business."

After lifting the knife so he could see it, he decided to keep it moving. I saw him looking at me through his rearview mirror. I hoped he didn't write down my license plate number.

Within the hour, I was at Clinton's apartment. He was already outside waiting for me. I couldn't believe that his hair had been washed, and even though his shorts were dirty, they were cleaner than the ones he had on yesterday. His skin remained ashy. I would help him take care of that real soon.

"Good morning," he said, opening the passenger's side door to my car. "You are right on time."

"So are you. I appreciate that, especially since we have a lot to do today. Is Velma okay with you leaving?"

"Not really, but what else am I supposed to do? She's always fussing about me not having any money, and then when I find ways to make money, she's still fussing."

"No offense, but what does she bring to the table? Does she even have a job?"

"Nah, she's been looking for work too. The struggle is real out here, and minimum wage just ain't cutting it."

"I know, but something is better than nothing. You would agree with that, wouldn't you?"

All he did was shrug his shoulders. It was pretty obvious that he had a lazy trick at home who wanted him to bring in the cash while she sat on her butt doing nothing.

"I agree, but a lot of the jobs paying minimum wage want to work you like a slave. Velma needs some light work. We just found out that she's six weeks pregnant. I don't want her working too hard."

I didn't bother to comment. I worked up until I was eight-and-a-half months pregnant with Kendal. And then, two weeks after she was born, I was back at work again. I just didn't buy his excuse for her not working. But, it didn't matter to me anyway. As long as he was willing to work, I was fine. I was going to let him build shelves for my closets, and then ask him to be my new standby man.

"Congrats on the baby. Is it your first child?"

"Nah, I have a son who is sixteen years old. I haven't seen him in years though. His mother and me don't get along. She kept him from me when he was little, and the last time I saw him was when I got out of prison."

"I'm sorry to hear that. I have a fifteen-year-old daughter who will be sixteen next week. I couldn't even imagine my life without her."

This time, Clinton didn't respond. I figured he was probably thinking about his son. I changed the subject.

"Are you hungry? If so, we can stop to get something quick to eat."

"I'm not real hungry, but some coffee and a donut would be nice."

I stopped at the nearest Dunkin' Donuts to get Clinton what he asked for. I ordered a bagel sandwich for myself. We ate in the car, while continuing to make small talk with each other. I was surprised to learn that we were the same age, and it intrigued me that he seemed well educated. He said that he'd gotten a degree while in prison. He also admitted that being there had changed his whole perspective on things.

"You keep asking all of these questions about me," he said. "But what's up with you? Do you work, have a man . . . what?"

"I do work, but I'm on vacation right now. I was once married; unfortunately, things didn't work out. Since then, I've been dating here and there. Nothing serious, though."

"I'm surprised to hear that. I figured a woman as fine as you are would have multiple men. Since that ain't the case, I assume your divorce was rough on you."

"Yeah, it was. I don't care to go into details, but I will say that I'm glad the marriage is over."

Clinton didn't say much else after that. The only time he spoke up was when we got to my house.

"Nice," he said as I pulled in the driveway. "I like the landscaping. You don't need me to take care of your yard at all."

"I have a lawn care service that takes care of that faithfully for me. But I assure you that I can use your help for other things."

We got out of the car, and when I unlocked the front door, we went inside. I gave Clinton a quick tour of the upper level, as well as the basement. It was empty, but through his eyes, he could work wonders.

"This basement is huge. You could have a bar area over there, and a movie theater right where we're standing. You even have room for a wine cellar, if you would like something like that."

"I would, but we'll have to talk about redoing the basement another time."

I walked up the stairs swaying my hips from side to side. I couldn't help but to wonder what Clinton was thinking as he walked behind me.

"The truth is," he said, "your place is already hooked up. I don't know how much work you think is needed in here, because other than your basement, I don't see many areas that need improvement."

"There are a few things. Come on and let me show you what I'd like for you to do with the closets."

I took Clinton to Kendal's closet first. It was thick with clothes, shoes, and purses that I'd gotten from Macy's. My discount was very beneficial. There was no question that when it came to clothes, we didn't need more.

"Wow. There's a lot of stuff in here," Clinton said as he turned in circles. "I would need you to clear out this closet so I can measure it. I have an idea about how I can stack the shelves, and once I see your closet, I'll sketch a drawing so you can see my suggestions."

I showed Clinton my closet as well. He was in awe by all of the things I had. He referred to me as a shopaholic as we sat at the kitchen table, discussing his drawing and the cost. In a nutshell, he only wanted a hundred and fifty bucks. I was willing to pay him much more than that, but I didn't tell him yet because I wanted to see his work first. He offered to help me clean out my closet, and after he completed the measurements, we took a five-minute break before heading to Home Depot.

Clinton suggested renting a truck to haul all of the materials at once. I thought that would be a good idea too. But as we were loading up the wood, my cell phone rang. I saw Brent's number flash on the screen. I knew why he was calling, but I didn't feel like answering my phone right now. I continued to help Clinton, and thirty minutes later, we returned to my house. I offered to help Clinton, but he told me to move out of the way. He totally took charge. I was impressed. I had never seen a man work so hard and be so focused on a job. He came across as a real professional. I sat on the bed, watching TV and observing him as he got down to business. And when lunchtime came, I offered to make him something to eat.

"I'm good," he said, wiping across his sweaty forehead. "Just bring me something else to drink. I really want to finish as much of this as I can for you today."

"You don't have to finish all of it today, do you?"

"The sooner, the better. And if you want to help, you can start cleaning out your daughter's closet. That'll save me a lot of time. I can measure her closet before I leave today."

I went to the kitchen to get Clinton an ice-cold soda. After I gave it to him, I went into Kendal's closet to clear it out. Brent had already interrupted me three times, and when he called again, I finally answered.

"I'm really busy, Brent. For a man who doesn't want anything else to do with me, I don't know why you keep calling me."

"You know damn well why I'm calling you. Were you at my house today?"

I played clueless. "Why would I be at your house when you basically threw me out the last time I was there?"

"You left because you didn't like what I had to say. Now, getting back to what you did to my wife's car today, stop the foolishness, please. I'm getting cameras installed today. If either of us catch you on our property, we will not hesitate to shoot."

"Listen, fool. I don't know what you're talking about, but please don't call me making threats.

If someone did something to her car, I suggest you go look for one of those thugs who live in your neighborhood. Because here's the truth, Brent. If you continue to harass me, I will call the police and have you arrested. I'm not going to put up with this mess from you or from your wife. Stop calling me, and go get a life."

This time, I hung up on him. I felt good about it too, and even though I lied, I thought my words were very convincing. I did, however, have to be careful. The last thing I needed was to be caught on camera, doing something that I had no business doing. Then again, I had every right. I smiled, wondering if he would still be upset with me when he saw me tonight. During our relationship, I introduced him to a live pool hall that had excellent food. Sometimes, Brent went without me to drink beer and hang out with his friends. I couldn't wait to walk through the door with my new man by my side.

Chapter Six

Several hours later, Kendal came home from school. Clinton was still there; he was almost finished with my closet. He said it would probably take him a day and a half to finish mine, but since he had been working his butt off, it would get done today. Simply put, I loved it, even though this wasn't supposed to be part of the plan. Kendal and I stood at the doorway, looking inside.

"Wow," she said. "It's amazing what he's done to your closet."

Clinton smiled and paused for a moment to greet Kendal. "Thank you, young lady. I'll be doing the same thing to your closet too, as soon as you and your mother get it all cleared out for me."

"Really?" Kendal said with excitement in her voice. "You're going to do mine like that too?"

Clinton nodded. I could tell that Kendal's compliment made him feel good.

"Yes, he's going to do yours too. I already cleared everything out. Your room is a mess. You may have to sleep on the couch tonight, because your clothes are all over your bed."

"That's fine with me. I've been trying to organize my closet for a looooong time. Thanks for having it done for me."

"Don't thank me, thank Clinton. He's the one putting in all the hard work."

Kendal laughed, so did Clinton. "Thank you, sir. I really appreciate it."

"No problem. Now, if you ladies don't mind, I need to get finished."

Kendal and I went to the kitchen. She sat at the table to do her homework, while I started on a quick meal for us to eat.

"How was school today?"

"Good."

"Good as in great or just okay?"

She sighed. "It was good, Mama. What else do you want me to say?"

"No issues? Is anyone else bothering you?"

"Nope. Everything is fine."

Kendal said the same thing every time I asked her about school. There had to be more to it than just "good," but I didn't know how to get much more than that out of her.

The Hamburger Helper was done in twenty minutes. I fixed her a plate, and then I told her that I would be leaving shortly to take Clinton home.

"Okay. Who is he anyway?" she asked. "Someone you're dating or someone you hired to do the job."

"He's someone I hired to do a few things around the house for me. Is there anything else you want done?"

"Why don't you have him finish the basement? I would love to move my room downstairs. I need more privacy."

"Girl, please. You have all of the privacy you need. And if you really need more privacy than what you already have, I guess you'll be moving in with your whack father then."

"Mama, don't even go there with him. You always gotta throw him up in our conversations, and just so you know, I haven't spoken to him in a while."

"I don't want to know because it's not any of my business. But just in case you happen to speak to him, tell him to send you some money for your birthday. You'll be sixteen next week. I guarantee you that he won't send you a dime."

Kendal shrugged. "Oh well, I guess it matters to you more than it does to me."

I could tell that she was getting irritated, so I dropped the conversation. I returned to my room, where Clinton was drilling away and almost done.

"You did not have to do all of this in one day. I know you're tired and hungry as well."

"I'm not tired, but I am a little hungry now."

"I made some Hamburger Helper, but I'm taking you to get some of the best wings in town. They also make good drinks too. Do you drink alcohol?"

"Not really, but on special occasions I do. The wings sound good, though."

"Okay, then wings it is. By the way, the closet looks amazing. I never thought it would look like this, and I'm just as excited as my daughter is."

"I'm happy to hear that. I'll be done in about ten or fifteen more minutes. I still need to measure your daughter's closet too."

"Why don't you wait until tomorrow? You've done enough already, and it's getting late."

"Yeah, you're right. And I haven't even called Velma yet. I'm sure she's worried about me."

"You can use my phone to call her. Just let me know, okay?"

He nodded, then got back to work. And as he predicted, he was finished in fifteen minutes. I stood in the doorway with towels, a brush, shampoo, and soap.

"Thank you so much, Clinton. I wasn't sure if you wanted to wash up before we go have dinner, but I figured you would, since you've been sweating all day."

"I surely would like to wash up, but my clothes are kind of—"

"Give them to me. I'll wash them for you real quick."

"No, I wouldn't want you to do that."

"I insist. It makes no sense for you to take a shower, and then put your dirty clothes back on. I can do a quick wash and dry. It shouldn't take more than thirty or forty-five minutes. While you wait, you can call Velma to let her know what's up."

Clinton agreed with my plan. He removed the items from my hand and went into the bathroom. After he removed his clothes, he stuck his hand out the door and gave them to me. Thankfully, his boxers weren't included. I put his clothes in the washing machine, and then returned to my room. I could hear Clinton singing while taking a shower. His voice was pretty good. It sounded like Maxwell's voice, but not quite.

As Clinton continued to shower, I looked for something to wear tonight. I found a casual dress that was made of jean material on the bottom and a tank at the top. It flared a bit and cut right above my knees. I grabbed my sandals that had a small heel. And just so I could be ready by the time Clinton was done, I went into the other bathroom to change. Once I was done, I removed his clothes from the washer and put them in the dryer. Kendal was awfully quiet, so I checked on her. She was still sitting at the kitchen table. Instead of doing her homework, she was texting someone.

"Are you finished with your homework?"

"Yes, Mama, I am."

"Okay. Just checking."

I headed back to my bedroom, and to my surprise, Clinton was sitting on my bed with a towel wrapped around his waist. His chest was carved nicely, and a huge cross with praying hands was tattooed on it. His hair was thick with waves. He seriously looked like a new man. His eyes searched me up and down before he stood.

"I didn't mean to sit on your bed, but—"

"No problem, Clinton. I just put your clothes in the dryer. They should be dry soon."

I went into the bathroom to get some lotion. After I gave it to him, he thanked me.

"I feel like I'm at a spa. That shower was everything. I almost fell asleep on that seat."

"I hope the water pressure wasn't too much. I like it high like that, but my daughter can't stand it."

"No, I loved it. Real nice. Thanks again."

He squeezed lotion in his hand and started to rub his chest and arms. I didn't want to stand there and watch, so I left the room to check on his clothes. They needed about five or so more minutes. I waited until they were done, and then I went back into my bedroom where Clinton was now standing and putting lotion on his feet.

"Here are your clothes." I laid them on the bed. "By the way, you have a nice voice. I thought Maxwell was in there instead of you."

He laughed. "Yeah, right. That compliment will not make me give you a discount on that closet."

"Maybe not, but you definitely earned a big tip."

I opened my purse, pulling out $300. When I reached out to give the money to him, he looked at it.

"Nah, that's too much. I said a hundred and fifty for both closets."

"I know what you said, but I feel as if you deserve more."

He didn't argue with me. Just thanked me and took the money before going back into the bathroom to put on his clothes. Ten minutes later, he came out looking brand new. I was now ready to go where I knew Brent would be chilling at tonight. If his wife happened to be with him, too bad.

On the drive to the pool hall, Clinton asked if he could use my cell phone. He called Velma. When he told her he had just got finished and was on his way to get something to eat, I could hear her yelling at him through the phone. All he did was suck his teeth. He didn't even respond, and after she was finished, I guess she hung up on him. He gave the phone back to me. I wondered why he was even putting up with her crap. He was too nice looking to be with her anyway, and pregnant or not, she was out of control. If her man was outside of the home making money, why was she tripping? I wanted to ask him so many questions about his relationship with her, but it really was none of my business.

"Sounded like she was upset with you," I said. "Would you like for me to take you home?"

"No, I'm fine. I haven't eaten much all day, so I'm definitely going to get me something to eat. I'll get her something and take it home to her."

I started to say something negative, but I decided against it. My mind switched to Brent, so I pressed on the accelerator to get to the pool hall faster.

Once we arrived at the pool hall, I saw Brent's car parked in its usual spot. I entered the place with a wide smile on my face. Clinton walked closely behind me. A band was playing some reggae music and thick smoke filled the air. Some people were sitting by the bar getting high. Others played pool or were there watching a basketball game. There was a small dance floor, so some people were on their feet dancing. Clinton and I sat at a bar that sat in the middle of the floor. Several people surrounded it, and the two bartenders behind it were very busy.

"How often do you come here?" Clinton said loudly as he leaned in closer to me.

"Not every week. Maybe once or twice a month. They have good drink specials, and like I said, the wings are delicious. All of their food is good. If you like fried shrimp, they have that too."

"I may take some of those home to Velma. She likes shrimp more than I do. I'll try the chicken."

"Okay. As soon as the bartender comes over this way, I'll order for us."

Clinton nodded while looking around the room. There were numerous decent-looking women in the place, but he didn't seem to give any of them a second look. I even noticed two of the women smiling at him. Either he didn't see them, or he pretended not to. I barely kept his attention on me, but maybe I hadn't noticed because I was too busy taking peeks at Brent who was sitting on a stool by one of the two pool tables next to a wall. I didn't see his wife with him, but I did see three of his friends who he often came here to meet. He definitely hadn't seen me yet, but it wouldn't be long before he did.

The woman bartender came over to us, asking what we were drinking.

"I'll take an Amaretto Sour, and you can get a Bud Light for my friend here," I said. "We would also like to order two large orders of wings with seasoned fries."

"Ranch or blue cheese?"

"I'll take Ranch. Is that okay, Clinton?"

"That's fine," he said, looking over the menu. "And if you wouldn't mind adding a shrimp box to go, I'd appreciate it."

"Do you want to order it now or wait until after you eat?"

"You can place the order later. Thanks."

He sure did take care of Velma—I remained puzzled. The bartender walked away, returning shortly after with our drinks.

"Go ahead and mix me up another Amaretto Sour. I'm sure I'll be done with this one in no time."

The bartender nodded, then walked away.

"Are you sure you want to do all that drinking?" Clinton asked. "You don't want to get a DUI, do you?"

"Two drinks won't kill me." I tossed the drink back, guzzling half of it down. "Besides, it takes more than just this to get me drunk."

Clinton put the bottle of beer up to his lips to take a sip. He continued to look around, as if he was intentionally trying to ignore me. I needed his attention focused on me, so I started talking about what a great job he'd done with the closet.

"I can't wait to get home and put everything in place. I don't know if I will do it tonight, but maybe tomorrow while you're working on Kendal's room."

"Yeah, why don't you wait until tomorrow? It's been a long day. I'm sure you'll be tired when you get home. Plus, you have to come pick me up early in the morning again."

I looked over his shoulder. That's when I saw Brent looking in my direction. Just to be sure that he saw me, I stood and leaned in close to Clinton's ear.

"The music is too loud. I didn't hear everything you just said. What time did you want me to pick you up?"

"Seven or eight is fine. And don't be surprised if Velma be standing outside with me tomorrow, wanting to go."

I giggled as if he'd said something ridiculously funny. My hand even touched his shoulder, and my breast was close to his arm.

"She wouldn't go there, would she?" I said.

My laughter caused Clinton to laugh too. "Uh, yeah, she would. Then again, she's pretty upset with me for not calling her today. When she's mad at me, she distances herself."

"Really?" I held my chest, pretending to be shocked. It looked as if Clinton and I were in a funny, yet interesting conversation. From the corner of my eye, I could see Brent coming our way. Without saying one word, he walked right behind me. I was sure that he had taken a look at Clinton, who was now focused on me.

"I would probably do the same thing," I said. "She's just trying to protect what's hers. You know how us women are."

"Yes, I do." Clinton chuckled, then took a sip of his beer. The bartender came back with my other drink. She let us know that our order had been placed. I thanked her, and she walked away.

I remained close to Clinton. He didn't seem to mind, and my flirty behavior got his attention.

"You are going to love these wings, trust me. And I bet any amount of money that you're going to beg me to bring you back here."

"What makes the wings so good? I mean, I've had all kinds of wings before."

I put the tip of my finger between my lips and sucked it. "It's the sauce. The sauce is perfect."

Clinton smiled, and just as I got ready to take a seat, Brent walked up. He looked at Clinton, then turned his attention to me.

"Since you hung up on me earlier, I didn't get a chance to finish what I had to say. Let it go, Abby. Please, let it go."

My face twisted. My brows were arched inward. "No, Brent, you need to let it go. Now, if you don't mind, I'm enjoying my evening with a friend. If you have anything else to say to me, please find another day or time to say it. Now isn't the appropriate time."

He cocked his head back, appearing taken aback by my tone. It was that or either he was jealous that I was there with someone else.

"You're right. It's not the appropriate time, but since you're here, I couldn't resist. If one more thing happens, shit is going to hit the fan. I hope you understand that I'm not playing with you."

Clinton's face was already tight from Brent's tone and his abrupt interruption. He looked past Brent to speak to me. "Is everything okay? He's being kind of rude, ain't he?"

"Everything is fine. This is just one of my bitter ex-boyfriends who seem to have a difficult time letting go."

"What?" Brent shouted. "Give me a goddamn break. *You're* the one who can't let go, and if you come by my house again, I'm calling the police."

I remained calm. He was the one standing there, looking like a fool. The people around us were looking at us, probably wondering what in the hell was going on.

I lifted my hand, putting it in front of his face. "Brent, please get away from me. I don't know what's up with your threats, but you really need to stop."

Clinton stood and intervened. "I don't know what's going on either, but this is not how you need to conduct yourself when you're speaking to a lady. We were in the middle of a conversation, before you interrupted. Maybe you should give her a call tomorrow to discuss what is troubling you. Or you can possibly take her advice and just leave her alone."

I had barely seen Brent upset or use foul language when we were together. This was a whole new Brent I was seeing, and it wasn't a good look for him.

"Fuck your advice and hers. She knows what she's been up to. All I can say is, she's been warned."

He walked away mad as hell. I loved every bit of it, but Clinton wasn't too pleased. "Maybe we should just get our food and go. I don't want any trouble, and you shouldn't be in the presence of an ex-boyfriend who can't control himself."

"I agree, but I don't want to run from him. He refuses to let go of our relationship. It's been over with for almost three months now."

"Well, you know how some fools are. They don't want to let go. He seems like the type, and you should be real careful."

I told Clinton that I would be. I also told him that I wanted to leave as soon as our food came.

"I appreciate you taking up for me but I don't want you to get involved, in case he comes back over here. We can eat in the car. As for Velma's food, maybe you can share some of what you have. Or I can stop by a fast-food joint so you can get her something."

"That would be nice. She likes Panda Express."

I really didn't want to stop and get her anything, but Clinton had done a good deed for me today. I didn't have to pay him one dime to stand up for me, and at this point, I wasn't going to ask him to pretend to be my man. I would just make sure Brent continued to see us together. That seemed to upset him more than he would ever admit.

Several minutes later, our food came. I asked the bartender to bag up everything, and after she did, I paid for the drinks and food. Clinton reached in his pocket and gave her a tip. He also paid for Velma's food at Panda Express. And after I pulled away from the drive-thru window, he tore into the wings I'd purchased at the pool hall.

"These are good, but I have to say that I've had better."

The truth was, I'd had better too. The purpose for going to the pool hall was not for wings. "I can't believe you said that. Those wings are the bomb. And please tell me where there's another place in St. Louis with wings like that."

"It's about a mile or so from where I live. I may have to take you there one day, just so you can see for yourself. Again, I'm not saying these wings are bad. The sauce just needs to be a little spicier for me. I like spicy food."

"I do too. And I'll take you up on your offer, whenever you're ready to take me there."

We laughed, and within minutes, we were at Clinton's apartment. Velma was standing outside talking to another woman. This time, she had on a sweat suit and her hair was in a ponytail with a big puffball in the back. Clinton turned to me with a blank expression on his face.

"Thanks for the wings. I'll see you around eight tomorrow morning. Something tells me this is going to be a long night."

"Maybe so, because she doesn't look too happy. How about I pick you up around noon? Get some rest and I'll see you at noon."

"Okay, cool. See you then."

Clinton could barely get out of the car before Velma came up to him, hooting and hollering about how long he'd been gone. She pointed her finger at his head. "See, nigga, you play too fucking much. You couldn't even call me?"

I didn't want her to say anything to me, so I drove off, looking in my rearview mirror. She was all up in Clinton's face. He ignored her and walked inside. I hadn't a clue what was up with that relationship. It was one that puzzled the heck out of me.

I was happy to be home, but to my surprise, as soon as I got out of the car, Brent's car came speeding down the street. He hurried out of it to catch me before I went inside.

"Are you ready to talk to me like you got some sense?" he yelled. "You know damn well that you flattened Lajuanna's tire. Who else did it but you, Abby?"

I crossed my arms, stepping a few inches back because he was too close. "How many times do I have to tell you that I had nothing to do with the damage to her car? If I did, you would know all about it. As would she. Now, good night, Brent. Go home and enjoy some quiet time with your wife."

I started to walk away, but he tightly grabbed my arm. I snatched away, but he grabbed it again, holding it tighter than he'd done before.

"I don't know what has gotten into you, but you're traveling down a dangerous path," he barked. "And—And when did you start dating somebody else? Were you fucking him while you were fucking me?"

I answered by spitting in his face. That surely made him release me, but he responded with rage. He shoved me backward, causing me to fall hard on my ass.

"Don't you ever do that shit to me again!" he shouted. "What in the hell is wrong with you, huh?"

I laughed after seeing him so unhinged. "What's wrong with *me?* You mean, what's wrong with *you.* I told you to stay away from me, Brent. You made your choice, so why are you still calling me and coming over here. I don't get this, and who I'm fucking is none of your business."

He pointed his finger at me. "I have a bad feeling about you. I want you out of my life, and I do not believe it was a coincidence that you were at the pool hall tonight."

I got off the ground and wiped my scraped knee. My face was scrunched. My feelings were quite bruised because every time he said it was over, I felt anger inside.

"In case you forgot, *I* was the one who told *you* about the pool hall. *I* used to go there way before you ever knew about that place. I'm not going to stop going places because you want me to. I'm not going to stop fucking who I want to, and to answer your question, hell, yes, I was seeing him at the same time I was seeing you. I just didn't want to choose, so I didn't."

Brent caught me off guard when he grabbed the front of my shirt, gathering it in his hand. He pushed me back, this time against my car. His other fist was tightened, and his eyes narrowed as he spoke through gritted teeth.

"You're a whore." His spit sprayed in my face. "A fucking whore who better stay the hell away from me and my wife if you know what's good for you."

He yanked me forward, then slammed me against the car before releasing my shirt. The real Brent had finally shown. I never thought he would put his hands on me, but there he was showing every bit of his ass. His finger was pressed against my temple.

"I don't know why I ever got involved with you. It's too late to have any regrets, but fuck you, Abby. Have a nice life with your other man, and tell him to stay the hell away from me too." He pushed my head with his hand, then walked back to his car.

I yelled out to him. "Wimpy bastard! Got your feelings hurt, didn't you? How does it feel? Feels good, doesn't it? Now you want to come here and accuse me of doing something that I didn't do! Go to hell, Brent, and take your hooker-looking-ass wife with you!"

He ignored me, got in his car, and sped off.

My body was aching from him pushing me on the ground and shoving me against the car. I was sure there were visible bruises, and surely enough, I saw them when I went inside and took a shower. I took pictures of my injuries, but waited until morning to go to the emergency room and get a sling for my arm. I guess he was too stupid to realize that he had really screwed up. The evidence I would use against him was starting to pile up.

Chapter Seven

When morning came, my body was sore all over. My head was banging too, and after I took two aspirins, I put on some clothes. Kendal was already dressed for school, so we headed out together.

"Do you want me to drop you off at school?" I asked.

"No, I'm taking the bus." Her mood was somber.

"What's wrong with you this morning?"

"I didn't get much sleep last night. Kept tossing and turning, and then I heard a lot of commotion going on outside. Who were you talking to? Brent?"

"Yes, that was him. He's having a difficult time letting go, so we had a little confrontation. Sorry about that."

"No problem. As long as you don't start seeing him again. You need to let him move on."

I smiled, then reached into my purse to give Kendal some lunch money. My shoulder was stiff, and my body ached even more as I extended my hand to her.

"Here's some lunch money. And please don't worry so much about my past relationship. Brent and I are done. Meanwhile, Clinton is coming back over today to get started on your closet. I'm not sure if he's going to finish today, but I don't see why not."

A smile appeared on her face. "That's great. I saw your closet and was like daaang. He really did a good job. And he's kind of cute. You should hook up with him and leave Brent alone for good, Mama. I doubt that it's really over. If it was, he wouldn't have been here last night."

"I'm not going to keep saying the same thing over and over again. Now, bye, Kendal. Have a good day, okay?"

She walked off to go catch the bus. I waited until it came, and then I drove myself to the emergency room. When all was said and done, I pretended as if I was hurting real bad and left with a sling on my right arm. As soon as the nurse left the room, I lifted my phone, taking a picture of my arm in the sling.

Since I didn't have to pick up Clinton until noon, I made a stop to put some fear in Brent. It was almost ten o'clock. I assumed he was in class teaching. I knew the woman, Sarah, who worked at the front desk. She waved at me, questioning why I was there.

"Brent left his keys at my place this morning," I said to her. "I also need to give him something else."

"Go right ahead," she said. "You already know where his classroom is."

I surely did, and with my high heels on, a tight skirt, and with my hair looking fly, I marched down the long hallway with a sling on my arm. A .22 caliber pistol was tucked inside of it, and if he said the wrong thing to me today, I sure as hell would use it.

Before going inside of his classroom, I looked through the windowpane. Brent was in front of the classroom with a yellow shirt on, navy pants, and black shoes. A tie was around his neck, and his bald head was cleanly shaven with a shine. Glasses shielded his eyes, and his goatee was trimmed. He definitely looked like an intelligent teacher. The classroom was filled to capacity with mostly teenage white students, only two black. They were tuned in to him speaking with a book in his hand. But when I pulled on the door, many of their heads shifted in my direction. So did his. He was stunned.

"Don't mind me," I said, looking at him. "Then again, you should. And while you're in here teaching class, maybe I should teach them a thing or two, as well, especially the young ladies."

Brent stood stone-faced as I walked up to the chalkboard and started to scribble on it with chalk. "Rule number one," I said out loud. "Do not date men who abuse you and treat you like crap. Two, do not date men who are married. Three—"

"That's enough," Brent hissed as he walked up to me. "Get out before I call security."

"Three, do not date men who make threats and who want to play the victim, when they're the ones who screwed you over."

I turned to the kids who all looked as if they were in shock. No one blinked, no one moved. That was, until Brent grabbed my arm again. I immediately lifted my sling, just so he could see the pistol inside. He slowly backed away with bugged eyes.

"Uh, boys and girls, I want you all to get out of your seats and exit now. No questions, just do it."

It didn't take long for chaos to erupt. Books were slamming, desks screeched on the floor, and there was a lot of pushing and shoving going on.

"Get the hell out of my way," one student shouted. "You guys are moving too slow."

"She has a knife or something. Oh my God!"

Brent stood nervous as he watched his students trying to exit from one door. They panicked as they walked by me, but I wasn't there to cause any of them harm.

"Call security, the police, or whomever you'd like," I said to Brent. "I have evidence that *I'm* the one who was battered. I had to let you know how serious this is for me, and if you ever put your hands on me again, you *will* pay with your life."

The bell rang, and it wasn't long before the hallways filled with students from Brent's class, along with students from other classrooms as well. Brent stood speechless. He wasn't sure if I was going to blow his damn brains out or not. The fear in his eyes made me smile.

"Don't be afraid," I whispered. "I love you too much to kill you. Love you too much to let you go too, so we *will* meet again."

I blew him a kiss before leaving. I wasn't sure if he would contact the police or not, but as I rushed through the crowd of students, some of them pointed me out to other students. I hurried to my car, fleeing before more trouble ensued.

Chapter Eight

Clinton had just gotten started on Kendal's closet when the police arrived. I suspected that they would come to my house, but with my car parked in the garage, I didn't answer the door. Clinton asked me what was going on.

"Last night, my ex came over and started harassing me," I said as the doorbell rang again. "He also put his hands on me, so I contacted the police. They said they would talk to him, so I guess they're back to tell me what he said. I don't feel like dealing with this crap right now. That's why I'm not going to my door."

"I don't blame you one bit. And as for your ex, you need to have him arrested. That's the only way you're going to stop him."

"Either that or stop him with a bullet. I've never thought about hurting anyone in my life, but last night was the final straw."

I put that out there just to see how Clinton would respond. There was a chance that I would pay him to *handle* a few things for me in the very near future.

"Don't do anything stupid like that. He's not worth it. You have too much to live for, and the last thing you want is to be locked away in a jail cell. Trust me, I know the feeling, and it ain't no place for a woman like you to be."

"You're so right. I know he's not worth it, but I'm very upset about all that has happened. I just wish he would leave me alone. And to think, *he's* the one married."

"That's how some married men are. They want to have their cake and eat it too. It's a good thing you ended things when you did."

I nodded, then looked out the window to see where the police officers had gone. There were two of them. They both were walking to their cars, getting ready to leave. That was a good thing, but I was sure they would be back.

Later that day, Kendal came home from school. Her closet was finished. She was ecstatic. "Oh my God," she said, looking inside of it with wide eyes. "I love it! This doesn't even look like my closet anymore. Thank you soooo much."

Clinton smiled from ear to ear, especially when Kendal gave him a hug. It made me feel good to see her so happy. If only I was too, but that was another thing.

"You're welcome," Clinton said, then turned to me. "We need to get going. I told Velma I wouldn't be too late today. I don't want to cause any problems, if you know what I mean."

He was starting to irritate me with his concerns for Velma. I told him to gather his things so we could go, and then I made it clear to Kendal that she was not to open the door for anyone.

"That includes the police. They want to talk to me about Brent. But do not open my door and tell them anything, okay?"

She agreed not to. After that, Clinton and I left. I was real quiet in the car, thinking about how I was going to handle this situation with the cops. Nobody but Brent saw the gun. It would be my word against his. I was going to stick to that lie, in hopes that it would be enough to keep me out of jail.

Clinton cleared his throat to snap me out of my thoughts.

"What's on your mind?" he asked. "You're awfully quiet over there."

"Just thinking about last night. I really don't want to talk about it, because it upsets me. And putting that aside, I did want to apologize to you for causing trouble between you and Velma. It's obvious that she doesn't like me, and I understand her concerns with her man being with a woman she doesn't like. The thing is, she doesn't really know me so—"

"So, it still doesn't matter. Velma doesn't like anyone but her friends she's known for years. Don't take it personal."

"She seems to like you a lot. And you seem to love her as well. I know the two of you have a baby on the way, but there seems to be many differences between the two of you. Meaning, are you two really compatible?"

"I think we are, but, sometimes, I question that myself. I just take it one day at a time with her. The last thing I be trying to do is upset her, especially since she's pregnant. So far, I haven't been successful. And it doesn't help that you're a very attractive woman."

His comment made me blush. "You're so sweet and nice. And there is no doubt that you have definitely upset her these past few days. I'm almost afraid to ask you to do any more work for me. That would mean you'll be spending more time at my place. I'm sure she wouldn't like that."

"She wouldn't, but I need all the work I can get. Besides, I enjoy being in the presence of another beautiful woman every day. What man wouldn't be happy about that?"

"Are you flirting with me, Mr. Clinton Jackson? If so, you shouldn't be doing that. Especially, since you have a sweet little ol' innocent and pregnant girlfriend at home."

He laughed. "I wouldn't say all of that, but pregnant she is. As for flirting with you, you know how we men do it. Regardless, I say those things to make you smile. You seem as if you got a lot going on, and I like to see you smile. Plus, I enjoy being around you. It feels good being in the presence of a woman I don't have to argue with."

I had enjoyed Clinton's company as well. And I needed him around more, to have a real effect on Brent. He bowled with his league on Thursday nights. I wanted to be there, but I didn't know how I could convince Clinton to go along with me.

"It's good to know that someone cares about my happiness," I said. "My ex surely doesn't, but it is what it is. By the way, I may need you to do a few more things for me in a couple of days. Until then, take good care of Velma and tell her I said hello."

I parked in front of Clinton's apartment. This time, Velma wasn't outside, but I saw him look around. He opened the door to get out of the car.

"I don't have a cell phone, but feel free to stop by if you need me Thursday. I can't think of any other place where I will be, other than right here."

"Will do, Clinton. Thanks again."

He exited the car, and without a doubt, I would be back on Thursday to get him. After I left his place, I did my daily drive-by at Brent's house. His car wasn't there again, but Lajuanna's car was. I wanted to get underneath her skin, so I parked my car in the driveway and went straight to the door. After I rang the doorbell, she yanked the door open and shot me a look that dared me to step forward.

"Bitch, what is *wrong* with you? How *dare* you come to my house, as if I invited you here."

"If Brent can come to my house when he wishes, surely I can come to his when I want to. I just came here to tell you that he's been harassing me. I don't know what he's told you, but he keeps calling me, keeps coming to my house, and when I saw him at the pool hall last night, he insulted the man I was with. They almost had a fight, but I told Brent he needed to back off. I'm just telling you this, because I know he's been lying to you about everything."

She released a deep sigh. "He may be, and I'm going to check him on that too. Wait right there while I go call him."

She walked away from the door, but seconds later, she returned with a bat in her hand, swinging it down low.

"You got one minute to get off my porch or else I'ma let your ass have it! I don't give a shit what Brent is doing. Don't you ever come to my house again!"

She stormed out the front door with the bat in her hand. I damn sure didn't want to get hit with it, so I rushed to my car, slamming the door after I got in. Lajuanna stared at me. I returned the evil glare right back at her.

"Move, bitch," she shouted. "Get out of my driveway, now!"

I guess I wasn't moving fast enough for her because the next thing I knew, she rushed up to my car, lifted the bat, and came crashing down on the hood with it. I witnessed a dent appear, as well as the paint chip. I revved up the engine and started to run that heifer over. But before another thought came to mind, she pounded my car with the bat again . . . and again. She came over to the driver's side, now, lifted the bat over my windshield, and cracked it into many pieces. A few shards of the glass fell inside of the car. That's when I backed out of her driveway with screeching tires. I almost crashed into a car that swerved to avoid hitting me. Lajuanna lifted the bat and continued to spew curses at me. I couldn't make out much of what she said, simply because the sound of my tires screeching drowned out her voice.

My heart was racing all the way home. I couldn't believe what kind of woman Brent was married to. It was now *game on* after what she'd done—I really meant it. The second I got home, I snapped photos of my car. I had so much damaging evidence against the two of them, it was almost laughable. Whenever the police came back this way again, I would certainly use the pictures in my favor.

A few days later, which also happened to be Kendal's birthday, I was arrested. We were getting ready to go meet some of her friends for dinner when the police arrived and arrested me. I told Kendal to contact her stupid father to come get her while handcuffs were put on me and I was taken to the police station to be booked. Kendal appeared nervous as ever as she watched the police car speed away. I hoped she did as she was told, and I couldn't stop thinking about her as the officer stood next to me with an attitude.

"I just don't understand how I can be arrested when no one has heard my side of the story."

The officer didn't respond. He snapped a photo of me in tears. I was asked to calm down, and minutes later, I was taken into a room where I was able to tell another officer, Officer Wayne, who happened to be sexy and black, what had been going on. I dug in my purse to show him the photos I had printed.

"This is so unfair," I said, smacking my tears away. "Brent has been the one harassing me. I tried to tell his wife about him, but she got angry and started pounding my car with a bat. It's in the shop getting fixed. I have to drive a rent-a-car to get around. Look at those bruises on my body and look at the damages to my car."

Officer Wayne flipped through the photos. I wasn't sure what he was thinking until he laid the photos on the table and looked at me.

"I'm more concerned about what happened at the school. Several students reported the incident to their parents. Mr. Carson has been suspended until an investigation is done. I was asked to bring you in and get your side of the story. What happened that day, and why did you go to the school with a gun?"

I cocked my head back. "*Gun?* I don't even own a gun. Who said I had a gun?"

"Mr. Carson did. None of the students mentioned it, but Mr. Carson said you had one."

"Mr. Carson is a liar. He will say anything to make himself look good. He's just upset that I ended things with him after he finally told me he was married. I would be lying if I said I wasn't upset with him for telling me about his wife, after he and I had been together for over a year. But what he's accusing me of is ridiculous. He needs to be the one arrested, and I should have gotten a restraining order against him the first time he put his hands on me."

"When was the first time he put his hands on you?"

I swallowed the lump in my throat and started to fake cry. Tears poured from my eyes. I was barely able to catch my breath. "He . . . He started abusing me about two months into the relationship. I didn't know what to do. I've never had a relationship with a man who put his hands on me, and I was scared, very scared, to report his actions. Had I known it would come to this, I now wish I would have said something a long time ago."

Officer Wayne's tone started to soften. "I know it's hard to speak up when things like that happen, but you have to report men who abuse you. Mr. Carson seems like a nice man, but so did Ted Bundy. Now, you have a situation where you must get an attorney to defend you or go before a judge yourself. I'll give you a summons to appear in court, but I can tell you that no judge is going to understand why you went on school premises to deal with personal matters."

"All I wanted to do was talk to him that day. I had just come from the hospital to have my arm looked at. I thought it was broken. I was upset, and I knew that he wasn't going to talk to me with his wife around. His job was the only place I could get him to listen to me."

"Tell all of that to the judge. I'm going to release you, but please do not miss your court date."

"I won't. I promise you I will be there."

He gave my photos back to me. "Be sure to have those with you, wear white, and bring any witnesses that you have."

I thanked Officer Wayne, and when he got up from the table, my eyes shifted right to the nice-sized print in his tight uniform pants. I wasn't sure if he'd seen the hungry look in my eyes, but he was one man who could definitely get it—right here and right now. Too bad he didn't seem to want it. He left the room, and in less than ten minutes, he came back with some paperwork for me to sign, and then I was free to go.

Unfortunately for me, I had to call a cab that didn't come until an hour later. I kept calling Kendal, but there was no answer. I hated to call Malik, but when he didn't answer I left a message, telling him I was on my way home, just in case Kendal was with him.

The second I got home, I could hear my telephone ringing off the hook. I rushed to it, and when I answered, the person on the other end hung up on me. After that, my cell phone rang. I answered that as well, and yet again, the unknown caller hung up. I suspected that it was either Brent or his wife trying to see if I was home. I guess they figured I would be locked up for days. Maybe I would have been, but the officer I spoke with seemed real nice. He advised me to get a lawyer, but I didn't need one to make my case for me. I was prepared to throw everything that I could at Brent, and then some.

Now that I was home, I waited to hear back from Kendal or Malik. I finally reached him after calling his phone over and over again.

"Why do you keep calling me, woman? I was at the casino and couldn't hear my phone. What is so damn important?"

"I thought Kendal was with you. I guess not."

"Why would Kendal be with me, especially when she's always with you?"

"Because something important came up. And since it is her sixteenth birthday, I thought you would've picked her up and spent some time with her."

He was quiet. Asshole didn't even remember that it was her birthday. What a deadbeat.

"I . . . I'll call her next week to see if she wants to do something. Better yet, just tell her to call me."

I just hung up on him. Between him and Brent, I had my hands full.

Since Kendal wasn't with him, I was worried about where she had gone. I was now blowing her phone up. I even called her friend, Tammi, to see if she was with Kendal.

"We talked earlier, but she told me she would call me later. If I hear from her, I'll tell her to call home."

"Please do. I'm real worried about her. I have no idea where she's at."

I paced the floor, biting my nails and wondering where my child had gone. I knew she felt some kind of way after seeing me get arrested, and why didn't she call Malik like I told her to? I had a feeling inside that something was very wrong. I kept looking out the window, and when the young man who came to my door that day pulled his car in my driveway, I knew what was up. Kendal had been with him. This shit was getting out of hand, so I rushed to the front door, opening it. As the two of them were inside of his car kissing, I marched outside to let them know that I didn't approve.

"Kendal," I shouted, causing her to back away from him. "What in the hell are you doing?"

She hurried to get out of the car. The boy looked at me with wide eyes. "Didn't I tell you not to come over here again?"

He didn't reply, but Kendal did. "Mama, it's my birthday. What did you want me to do? Go to the police station with you?"

I wanted to choke her. Instead, I pointed to the door, ordering her to go inside. "*Now*, Kendal, before I hurt your feelings."

"You've already hurt my feelings by coming out here embarrassing me."

"Good! And I'm about to hurt them even more when we get inside." I looked at the boy again. "Out! Get out of my driveway and don't come here again. I have a feeling that you're too old to be with my daughter. If you come here again, I'll have you arrested."

That surely got his ass out of my driveway. Kendal went inside, huffing and puffing about how much I had ruined her day.

"You ruined your own day, sweetheart. I told you to call that fool-ass father of yours. Why didn't you call him?"

"I did call him, but he didn't answer his stupid phone. He doesn't have time for me, and neither do you. So I found someone who was willing to make time for me. Now, you're mad."

I walked toward the kitchen, just so we didn't have to yell at each other from a distance. "You're darn right I'm mad. Mad because you have no business riding around with that boy. You're only fifteen, and he looks as if he's nineteen or twenty something."

"I'm sixteen, thank you very much. And old enough to choose my own friends."

"Wow, sixteen. You're so grown," I said sarcastically.

Kendal rolled her eyes and plopped down in a chair. "Are you done yet?"

"Yes, I am. I'm done, and I'm leaving. I need to get out of here tonight. As for you, young lady, don't you leave this house and go anywhere else today. Got it?"

She'd already had her fun, so she acted as if she didn't care. I watched her go into her room and close the door. I listened to her on her cell phone, talking to someone about how much she hated living here with me. Kendal just didn't know how good she had it. Poor child didn't have a clue.

I left and drove around for a while, thinking about my chaotic situation. Kendal and I always managed to patch things up, but this situation with Brent still had me on edge. I didn't know why I couldn't just get over it and move on. I hated him so much, and what he had done to me took so much out of me. I found myself driving by his house again. This time, both cars were in the driveway. The lights were on. I wondered if he had gotten the cameras like he said he would. From a distance, I didn't see any cameras, but that didn't mean they weren't there. I parked my car almost a block away from his house. The closer I got, the more I checked my surroundings. If he had cameras, I surely didn't see them up close. He was probably just trying to scare me, but it would take more than his words to do that.

I tiptoed to the front window to look inside. The living room was dim. No one was in there. I then went to the side of the house to look into the dining room and den. A light was on in the den, and a few candles were lit in the dining room. Still, there was no sign of Brent and his wife. A crunching sound was underneath my feet as I stepped on a pile of leaves and made my way around back, to his bedroom window. Again, the lights were dim, but I could see the two of them standing and hugging each other near the bed. They were talking to each other. I wished I knew what they were saying. Brent was in his boxers, Lajuanna was in a pair of jeans and a bra. They laughed, and as she tried to walk away, Brent reached for her hand, pulling her into his arms. They kissed, and his hands lowered to cuff her healthy ass cheeks that looked perfect in those jeans. She playfully backed away from him, shoving his chest with laughter again. That's when he lifted her in his arms, carrying her to another room. I wasn't sure where they went into. I walked around to the other side of the house and saw them standing in the den. Another conversation took place, and minutes later, she left the room again. Within a minute, she came back with a shirt in her hand. She pulled it over her head, and I saw her pick up her purse from the table. She stepped forward to kiss Brent again, and the two of them walked toward the front door. I hurried to duck down, figuring she was leaving. From behind a bush, I saw her get into her car and back out of the driveway. I hoped that she wasn't going in the same direction as I was parked. I sighed with relief when I saw her go the other way. When I heard the door shut, I rushed back to the window. Brent opened the door to get a towel from the linen closet. He threw it over his shoulder, and I saw him crank up the volume on the radio.

He walked toward his bedroom again. I moved quickly to look in that window again. This time, I saw him remove his boxers and toss them on the bed. The towel was still thrown over his shoulder, so I assumed he was about to take a shower. I waited until he closed the bathroom door before I made my next move.

Getting into Brent's house was easy. He kept a spare key underneath a flowerpot on the porch. I hoped he hadn't removed it, and sure enough, when I moved the pot aside, there was the key. I stuck it in the lock. The door popped right open. As I walked inside, I could smell incense burning. Most of the rooms in the inside were dimly lit, but the kitchen light was the brightest. Soft music played throughout, and as I tiptoed down the hallway, taking myself to the bathroom, I heard Brent whistling. The water was running too. I wasn't sure how much time I had before his wife came back, but this was one time I was willing to take a big risk. I stripped naked and tossed my clothes on the bed. There was a comb on the dresser, so I combed my hair back, slicking it down with my hands. I took a deep breath before opening the door to the bathroom. The light was on, but I quickly turned it off.

"Yeah, I figured you would come back to get you some more," Brent said, as I heard the shower door slide over.

"Mmmm-hmmmm," was all I said, then moved my way toward him.

I stepped inside of the shower, our bodies were real close. Water rained on us, and I could already feel my coochie leaking. He lifted his hands to hold the sides of my face. And as he leaned in to kiss my lips, I wasn't sure if I should go for it all or just peck his lips. I quickly decided that a peck was good enough. Maybe for me, but it wasn't for Brent. He lifted me to his waist. I straddled my legs around him, my arms were around his neck. After he inserted his dick inside of me, my head dropped back. My mouth opened. I was excited to feel his strokes again. I wanted to tell him how he made me feel, but I waited. Waited until he touched my hotspot that made me release a satisfying moan.

"Mmmmm, you're so wet, and you smell so damn good," he said. "Why is your pussy so tight like this?"

If only I could tell him why. I didn't want him to get suspicious, so I lowered my legs, causing his steel to slip out of me.

"Wha . . . Where you going?"

I dropped to my knees to silence him. While holding his thick muscle with my hand, I began to slob and bob all over it. He could barely stand still. He dropped to the shower seat behind him, taking deep breaths. And when his hands started to roam in my hair, that was when the festivities were just about over. His fingers tightened in my hair, and he shot up from the seat like a rocket.

"Wha . . . who the fuck—"

Brent hurried out of the shower and flicked the lights on. I remained in the shower, where the warm water continued to pour on me. His eyes grew wide and wider.

"Are you fucking crazy?" he shouted. "How in the hell did you get in here?"

"Does that really matter? Calm down and let me finish what I started. You know you enjoyed it, Brent, so stop tripping."

With a tight face, he rushed out of the bathroom, threatening to call the police. I ran out of the bathroom, only to see him standing next to his dresser with the phone up to his ear. I snatched the phone and held it behind my back.

"I said calm down. All I want is for you to make love to me, like you used to do. Give me five minutes of your time, and then I'll leave."

Rage covered Brent's face. His eyes narrowed, and before I knew it, he charged me. I fell back on the bed, with the phone and my arms still tucked behind me. Brent and I tussled as he tried to take the phone from me.

"Give it here, you crazy bitch! You need help! Mental help because this makes no damn sense!"

I kneed him in the groin for calling me a crazy bitch. That got him to calm down, and as he held his goods, I reached into a drawer in his nightstand where I knew there was a pocketknife.

"I won't use this if I don't have to." I straddled myself on top of him as his eyes were squeezed together. Poor baby was in so much pain. I offered to help him. "Awww, let me take care of that for you. I promise that after I'm finished, you will feel so much better."

I held the knife near the center of Brent's chest. And as I lowered myself, I lightly bit into his hand, telling him to move it away from his goods. He slowly released his hand, and after I shoved it away from his dick, I covered the limp thing with my mouth. It took a few minutes, but inch-by-inch, his dick started to rise. He dropped his head back and kept taking deep breaths, as if he was trying to fight the feeling.

"Don't do this," he said in a whiny voice. "Stop this, Abby, please stop this. I . . . I don't want you anymore."

Hell, I surely couldn't tell. His dick had grown to new heights. I damn near sucked the skin off of it, and as my jaws tightened and my throat felt deeper and deeper to him, he was defeated. His semen sprayed my mouth, and there was plenty of it. I licked my lips and stood up. Brent attempted to sit up, but I held the knife in his direction.

"Stay. Don't move until I leave. That was good, baby. I wish we'd had more time in the bathroom, but maybe next time. Call me if you ever want to feel the tightness of my pussy again and get a whiff of my sweet-smelling perfume. As always, I'll be waiting on you."

I kept my eyes on Brent as I snatched up my clothes and reached for my purse. My phone was inside, so I pulled it out, hurrying to take a picture of him lying on the bed with a dripping wet dick. He appeared so stunned by my actions that, at first, he lay on the bed like a mummy. Taking the photo caused him to move, but, yet again, he was met with the knife.

"No, Brent. This was a good day. Let's not end it with blood splatter."

Fear was in Brent's eyes. He showed what a coward he was—he also showed what a weak man he was too. Our eyes stayed connected as I backed up to the door, and once he was out of my sight, I jetted out the front door, hiding behind a bush while hurrying into my clothes. I then pranced down the dark street, as if I was going for a relaxing walk. When I reached my car, I got in and sped off like a bat out of hell. I suspected that Brent was coming for me.

Chapter Nine

As usual, I was right. Brent was at my house on Thursday, knocking on my door. All I did was take a photo of him before he walked away. He called my cell phone, but I didn't answer. I waited until ten or fifteen minutes after he left, and then I headed to Clinton's apartment to see if he would go bowling with me. I was sure that was where Brent would be, and if he wanted to talk, he'd have to talk to me with my *new* man around. Hopefully, Clinton would be home when I stopped by. More than anything, I hoped he used the money I'd given him to clean himself up a bit.

I parked my car in front of Clinton's apartment. He was outside, sitting next to a man who looked high as hell. Clinton stood to greet me, and as I walked their way, I could smell marijuana smoke in the air. I coughed a bit to clear my throat.

"Hello, Clinton," I said.

"What's up? I've been waiting for you to come back down and holla at me. I thought you were supposed to get at me last week."

"I was, but something came up. I was just in the neighborhood, and I thought I would stop by. I need you to look at my basement for me, again, and let me know how much you would charge me to frame it. I can get someone to put up the drywall. I just need some specific ideas about how it should be framed."

"You know I can do that for you. I can put up the drywall for you too. That will be no problem at all."

"Great. Maybe you can come by sometime this weekend and look at everything for me. Meanwhile, I was on my way to the bowling alley. Would you and Velma like to go with me?"

He quickly shook his head. "I know Velma wouldn't, but I don't mind going."

"Where is she? Is she here?"

"She's upstairs watching TV, I think."

"Will she be okay with you leaving?"

Clinton looked at the man who was sitting in a lawn chair on the porch. "Cover for me, Ray. I'll be right back. Tell her I went somewhere with your cousin if she asks."

The man nodded. Clinton and I walked away. After he got in the car, I looked at the filthy tennis shoes he wore and the T-shirt that had food stains on it. His cargo shorts were nice, but he had to come a little better than this. As for his hair, it needed another cut too. I wasn't sure what he'd done with the money I'd given him, and I didn't hesitate to ask. He didn't hesitate to reply.

"Shit, I paid some bills with it. Rent was due, the electric was up for disconnection, and food is getting very expensive."

"I'm with you on that, but I wish you would have bought something nice for yourself. When is the last time you purchased something nice for you?"

"It's been a minute. I try to catch deals at the flea market. They be having some nice jeans, shorts, and shirts there. I haven't made my way over there yet, and besides, I'm fresh out of cash. The last thing I purchased was a bag of weed. That broke me."

"So, you get high?"

He turned his head, looking at me as if I had just called him out of his name. "Hell, yeah, I smoke weed. Everybody smokes weed. Don't you?"

"No, I don't. Am I supposed to?"

"Man, you are missing out. I don't do any of that other shit, but weed is a must."

"If you say so. I just wouldn't take my last dollars to purchase any. I'd rather have clothes, food, or a decent haircut instead of that. Speaking of haircuts, is there a place around here where I can get my hair trimmed?"

He looked at my hair and paid me a compliment. The truth is, I wanted him to get *his* hair cut. Maybe, just maybe, I would do the same.

"Your hair is always hooked up. It doesn't look like you need to go to the barbershop to me."

"I've been thinking about getting it trimmed low. A friend of mine has hers shaved off, and it looks real nice. Do you think that style would look nice on me?"

Clinton nodded. "You're a beautiful woman. Any style would look good on you."

He made me smile, then gave me directions to a barbershop that was several blocks away. Just my luck, there was a guy outside selling T-shirts. I pretended as if I wanted to purchase a few of them, and then I asked Clinton if he wanted one.

"Nah, I'm good. I don't want you spending your money on me."

"I'm not spending my money on you. You're going to repay me when you complete my basement. Pick out a few shirts you like. And if you see anything Velma may like, get her one too."

That surely got him looking through the shirts. They were two for twenty-five dollars, so he picked out one for him and one for her.

"Thanks," he said, putting on the clean shirt. "I owe you."

"Yes, you do. And I intend to get everything that is due."

He opened the door for me to enter the barbershop. I put my name on the short list to get my hair cut, and then I asked Clinton if he wanted to get his cut too, since we were there.

"Yeah, that's cool. Go ahead and put my name down."

Clinton and I waited about fifteen minutes before our names were called. And after all was said and done, I left the barbershop with my head trimmed low. Clinton got a sharp lining and trimming that made his hair, as well as his facial hair, look spectacular. The only thing he needed was shoes. I didn't trip because as soon as we got to the bowling alley, he would have to swap those out for bowling shoes.

"You really should keep your hair like that at all times," I said as I drove off. "You look so handsome, and if you don't mind me saying, you'll have any woman you want if you keep looking like that."

"I have the woman I want. Period. The end. She's it. Your cut looks nice too. I must say that I was a little skeptical, but you working that, mama."

His compliments could one day be very rewarding, but since he thought Velma was all that, and then some, I didn't push. Instead, I drove to the bowling alley, talking to him about what I wanted done to my basement. I actually wasn't going to have him do anything this time. I didn't want my basement finished, and eventually, I'd find a way to weasel out of it.

Clinton and I walked into the bowling alley together. It was crowded, but there were still open lanes. There were two or three leagues in the far corner. I knew Brent was in one of those groups. I asked the man behind the counter for a lane that was as close to them as possible.

"When is the last time you bowled?" I asked Clinton.

"Probably since the last time you smoked some weed. Which is never."

"Really? Why did you come with me then? I thought you knew how to bowl."

"I just wanted to get away from the crib. Been cooped up all week and I needed to get out."

I gave Clinton his pair of bowling shoes, then removed mine from the counter. We walked away to go to our lane. "Have you and Velma been into it again?"

"All day, every day. She likes to argue, but I'm good at ignoring her."

"If that works for you, so be it. I've just never known a man who likes to be yelled at all the time."

Clinton shrugged, refusing to say anything else about Velma. We put on our shoes, and as we sat next to each other, I showed him how the tally sheet worked.

"Okay," he said. "Are you going first or me?"

"I'll go first. You can watch how I do it. And if you look real careful, you just may learn something."

He laughed, and so did I. I stepped up, wearing tight jeans and a shirt that was cut at my midriff. My new hairstyle was the bomb—Brent's wife couldn't compete if she tried. I rolled the ball down the lane, but only knocked down seven pens. On my first attempt, a strike would've made me feel better. I pouted and pivoted to look at the busy groups of leagues bowling. I saw Brent sitting down, but he was indulged in a conversation with another bowler. Sooner or later, I was sure he would see me. Until then, I took another shot at knocking the pins down, but my second ball went into the gutter. I snapped my fingers.

"Shoot! I guess I'm a little rusty today."

"Sure," Clinton said, standing. "That's what they all say."

It was his turn. He stood with great posture, looking sexier than I ever thought he could. I loved to look at his smooth legs and toned calves. He rolled the ball down the lane with much power. And sure enough, on his first try, he got a strike.

"This is BS, and you know it," I said. "You already knew how to bowl, didn't you?"

He laughed, and I playfully punched his arm. Now that I was aware that he knew how to bowl, the competition was on. We were in a battle to win. I was going for all strikes, and so was he. Too bad, though, that he was winning. I pouted and rolled my eyes, after he got another strike.

"Don't be so bitter, li'l mama," he said. "The look doesn't suit you. Smile, be happy and be well."

Clinton chuckled, so did I. We were having so much fun that I finally took a moment to look Brent's way. And sure enough, his eyes were looking in our direction. I cut my eyes at him, and then I got back to my game with Clinton. Now that I knew Brent was looking, I was all over Clinton. I laughed as if we were having the best time ever. We also did a whole lot of trash talking about who would win the game.

"It damn sure won't be you," he said. "You are too far behind now. And after this strike, you can forget it."

Clinton released the ball, but before he did, I playfully jumped on his back to distract him. The ball rolled down the lane and went right into the gutter.

"Cheater," he said as I got down and backed away from him. "All you do is cheat, cheat, cheat! I can't wait until you take your turn. I'ma mess up your game too."

"That may have to wait. I need to run to the ladies' room real quick. I've been holding it for a while, so wait, okay?"

"Sure. Take your time."

I saw Brent looking at us time and time again. And just in case he was still watching, I made my way to the restroom. I didn't even have to go, but I washed my hands and dabbed just a little more gloss on my lips to make them shiny. When I exited the bathroom, Brent was right there waiting for me.

"Listen," he said, trying to keep a calm voice. "You and I need to talk. Can you go outside with me for a minute?"

"I honestly don't want to, because I don't—"

"Please. This is important. We have got to clear this up right now."

I cut my eyes at him and crossed my arms. "Sure. But make it quick, Brent. My boyfriend will be looking for me, if I'm gone too long."

Brent walked toward the exit sign that was only a few feet away. I followed. When we got outside, we stood next to the building. He was in front of me, while my back was against the wall.

"I seriously think you need to get some help," he said. "You're doing things that seem so out of character for you. I don't know if I just didn't know much about you or not. Nonetheless, the way you're acting is, is really scary. I'm afraid something bad is going to happen if you don't stop this."

I looked at him with a smirk on my face. "So, *I'm* the one who needs some help, even though *you're* the one who thought it was a bright idea to fuck with my head, make me love you, and then tell me to go to hell? No, Brent. *You're* the one who needs help. None of this would be happening if you hadn't done what you did. I'm just making you pay for hurting me, and once I feel as if you're really sorry for what you did, I'll fall back and leave you alone. The good thing is, my other man is taking my mind off you. So, you may get your wish. It just won't be any time soon."

"Well, it needs to be because my wife is getting real irritated with you. She's losing her patience, and she's to the point where she's talking about killing you. I don't want you to get hurt, so back off. Do it now, and if you need for me to say I'm sorry for how I treated you, I will say it. I'm sorry, okay? I should have handled myself a lot better than I did."

I clapped my hands. "That's wonderful, Brent. Thanks for the apology, but you're a little too late. If you're really sorry, drop the charges against me so I don't have to go to court. If you do that, then I'll really know you're sincere."

He swallowed, then looked down at the ground. His hands were in his pockets; he was in deep thought. "I can't do that."

"Why? Because your wife wants you to see it through, doesn't she?"

"Yes, so I can't back out of it."

I shrugged. "Well, I'll see you in court then. Next week, right? I hope she'll be with you, because my man will definitely be with me."

I walked away, leaving Brent outside with his thoughts. He yelled out, "Nice hair. The style looks good on you and on my wife as well."

I couldn't help but to fire back at him. "It probably does, but it's apparent that she has no idea how to fuck you and keep you. If she did, you wouldn't have allowed your dick to stay in my mouth. For the record, the fight you put up wasn't worth a damn."

I opened the door and went inside. When I returned to the lane where Clinton was, he asked what had taken so long.

"One of my girlfriends from high school was in the restroom running her mouth. I couldn't get away from her for nothing in the world."

Clinton laughed. We continued our game, and when it was over, he was the victorious one. He wouldn't stop boasting. Even when we got in the car, he continued to brag about how badly he had beaten me.

"Choose any sport," he said. "Even volleyball. I bet I can beat you at that too."

"Probably so because I do not like volleyball."

"Neither do I. You would probably beat me at that for real."

Clinton reached into his pocket. He pulled out a joint and instantly lit it. After he took a few puffs, he reached out to give it to me.

"Try it," he said. "It won't kill you, I promise."

"No, thanks. I've never done that, and I'm not about to start now."

"You don't have to start, just try it. It ain't no biggie. Besides, when you asked me to try bowling I did, didn't I?"

"There is no comparison, and you know it."

"I'll give you that, but try it anyway."

I was reluctant to try it, but after Clinton asked me again, I took the joint from his hand. I placed it between my lips and inhaled. The smoke filled my mouth.

"Inhale deeply," he said. "Real slow and let it kind of marinate."

I laughed, causing the smoke to blow out of my mouth. Clinton laughed too.

"See, that wasn't so bad, was it? You did good."

"Please. I don't feel a thing. Am I supposed to feel something?"

"Keep hitting that mutha. You'll feel it, soon enough."

I took another puff, then another. And by the time I reached Clinton's apartment, all I felt was drowsy. My eyelids were a little low, and my whole body felt light.

"What time are you picking me up this weekend?" Clinton took the last hit from the joint, then put the tip in my ashtray.

"I guess around noon. Will you be ready?"

"I'm always ready."

"Not always, Clinton. Because I assure you that you're not ready for this."

I leaned in his direction and placed my lips on his. They were thick and soft, just as I had imagined them to be. He didn't back away from my kiss, but when I forced my tongue in his mouth, that's when he did.

"Whoaaa," he said, looking at me. "No, I wasn't ready for that, and you, you already know what's up with me and Velma."

"I know, but I just wanted to see how soft your lips were. No harm in that, is there?"

Clinton sighed, then touched the knob to open the door. "If you only knew, man. I swear, if you only knew."

"Knew what? What are you talking about?"

"Nothing. Just don't do that again."

He was dead serious when he opened the door to get out. And sure enough, Velma was right there waiting for him. She came from out of nowhere, like a ghost or something, watching his every move.

"Where have you been?" she asked. "I thought you went somewhere with Ray's cousin?"

I got out of my car, not knowing if she had seen me kiss him or not.

"It was my fault, Velma. I had him come to my house and look at my basement. I didn't mean—"

Clinton cut me off. "Stop tripping," he said to her. "You've been fussing all damn week. I have a headache right now. Chill with that mess, 'cause you already know what's up."

"No, I don't know. But I do know I'm getting sick and tired of this slut coming over here. Every time I look up, she's coming to get you. If you ain't fucking around with her, pull your damn jeans down and let me see your dick."

My eyes bugged. She couldn't be serious, could she? Did she *really* want him to pull his shorts down so she could examine his dick? I was in total disbelief. More so when Clinton did it. Right outside, he lowered his shorts and let his dick fall into her hands.

"See? Nothing. Now what?"

She touched, flipped, turned, and squinted as she tried to find something on it. I had to look myself too. He was packing a load. No wonder she was acting a fool like she was. She definitely didn't want to share anything like that.

"Are you done yet?" Clinton said while holding his shorts.

"No, I'm not done." She looked at me. "Go! He doesn't want your business. Find someone else to do your basement. Don't come back here again, because I'm sick of seeing your face."

Clinton shook his head, turning to me as well. "Saturday at noon," he confirmed. "I'll be waiting for you to pick me up."

He walked off, and so did Velma. I got in my car, thinking about how crazy Velma was. She was nothing like me. Then again, maybe that's why she didn't like me. Maybe we had something in common in our own little special way.

Chapter Ten

When Saturday rolled around, I didn't worry about going to get Clinton. I was sure he would be disappointed, but my mind was focused on my court date on Monday, as well as on Kendal. She and I had settled our differences the other day, but when I went to her room this morning, she left a note on the bed, telling me that she had left to go stay with Tammi and her mother for a while. Said we needed a break from each other, because, according to her, things weren't working out here. I was so damn mad. I called Tammi's phone, and as my pitch rose, she gave the phone to her mother, allowing her to deal with me.

"Lower your tone, Abby," her mother, Barbara, said. "Kendal asked if she could move in with us for a while. I told her that I wanted to speak to you first. I left you several messages to call me, but I didn't get a return phone call."

"I don't know what number you've been calling because I haven't received one message from you. Kendal needs to come home right now. She and I can talk through whatever she claims she's going through."

"She doesn't want to come home, Abby. She doesn't like it there. I think it will do the two of you some good to be away from each other for a while. That's just my opinion."

"To hell with your opinion. I didn't ask for it, nor do I need it. You tell my daughter to come home right now! If she doesn't, she will never be able to come back here again."

"I honestly don't think she cares. Threatening her is not going to make her want to come home."

"Like hell it won't. I don't want to come over—"

"Listen, Abby, calm down. Just let her stay here for a few days. Then we can all get together next week and talk about what's been going on. Does that sound okay?"

"No, it doesn't, but you know what, Barbara? If she wants to stay there, fine. I'm not going to kiss nobody's ass, especially my child's who is just spoiled fucking rotten!"

Not wanting to hear anymore, I ended the call. Just who in the hell did Barbara think she was? I truly felt as though Kendal had betrayed me. I was so worked up that I needed a cigarette. I hadn't smoked in years, but things were starting to get hectic around here. If I had one of Clinton's joints, I would have smoked it. Instead, I drove to the store and got me a pack of cigarettes and a stick of gum. As I waited in line, a man behind me kept whispering, "Mmmmm, seeeexy. Damn, you look good. I only wish you were mine. Mmm, mmm, mmm."

I tried to ignore him by not turning around. I was clearly annoyed, and after I paid for my items, I left the convenience store. Unfortunately, he followed after me.

"Ay, ay, you with the big ol' booty. Don't you hear me talking to you?"

I was seething inside. I hated for a man to disrespect me in that manner. Did he really think I would turn around and start conversing with him? I kept it moving, but when he jumped in front of me, *that* got my attention.

"Damn, what's the rush? I was just trying to say what's up."

Talk about a thug, he was that, and then some. Pants hanging down low, eyes fire red from him being high, breath stinking, and lips were very crusty.

"You said what's up, now move on."

I walked around him, but that was when he grabbed my arm. He sucked his rotten teeth, and his eyes twitched as he narrowed them.

"You think you too good for me or something?"

"No, really, you're too good for me. I'm a crazy bitch. And if you don't let go of my goddamn arm, I'm going to reach for this gun down in my pants and blow your brains out."

Crime in St. Louis had gotten out of control. There was too many innocent people getting killed, and many of those crimes took place at gas stations and convenience stores. I didn't leave home without my pistol, especially at night.

He released my arm. "My bad. Have a nice night, li'l mama."

"You too, big brother."

I walked away, knowing that I had taken a risk by challenging him. He could have shot me dead right then and there. Thankfully, he didn't.

As I neared my vehicle, I saw that it was slightly leaning. I looked at my front tire. It was flat. My heart dropped to my stomach as I searched around for someone suspicious on the parking lot. I wondered if my tire had been slashed or if the air had simply come out of it. Something felt strange, so I kept on looking around. It didn't make sense that someone had been watching me; then again, I wasn't so sure. I finally bent down to look at the tire, but I didn't see any slashes or cuts. I did, however, see the dude who had approached me getting into his car. I waved my hands up high to flag him down.

"Hey," I said with a smile as he lowered his window. He was smiling too. "Hi. Would you mind helping me with my tire? It's flat, and I need someone to put the spare on. It's in the trunk."

He nodded and sucked his teeth again. "What's in it for me? I'll change it, but what you gon' do for me?"

"I'll go inside, buy you some soap so you can wash your nasty ass. Or maybe buy you some toothpaste so you can tackle that horrific breath of yours. Which one would you like?"

"Bitch, fuck you! Go in there and buy you some weave. Your bald-ass head looks shitty."

His comeback didn't even faze me. He sped off and damn near crashed his car into a utility pole. I shook my head, thinking about this bad day and night I was having. The upside was I'd finally come across a man who was willing to help me. He removed the tire, showing me a thick nail that had punctured it.

"You must have run over this," he said. "There's a little slash here too, but that could've come from glass or something else."

"Thank you," I said as he put the damaged tire in my trunk.

He pulled out the spare and squatted to put it on.

"I really appreciate this."

"No problem. Just be sure to get a new tire soon. Spare tires don't last long."

I thanked the man again. After he was finished, he went inside to wash his hands. I sat in my car, taking numerous drags from a cigarette that was tightened between my fingers. Today wasn't a good day for me. My anger had boiled over. I don't know why so many people kept on disappointing me, and this is what I got for being too fucking nice. I sped off the parking lot, almost hitting a car that was taking too long to exit the lot. As I swerved around it, I rolled my eyes at the woman who was sending a text message with her hands high on the steering wheel.

"Stupid bitch," I yelled.

She didn't hear me because my window was up. I sped down the dark road, swerving around cars that were going too slow, while continuously puffing on my cigarette to help calm my nerves. They were definitely rattled, and the more I thought about my court date tomorrow, I became so unhinged that I had to pull my car over and take several deep breaths. I clenched my chest, and as I counted out loudly, my heart stopped racing. I started to feel slightly better, thank God for that. As I pulled away from the curb, I hoped and prayed that my trip to the courthouse would lift my spirits.

***

The following day, I sat in a courtroom filled with people, waiting for the judge to call my name. There was no sign of Brent yet. I wondered if he was still coming. The judge had already made it clear that more detailed cases would be dealt with last. He seemed okay, until a black man stood there with an attitude that pissed him off.

"Sir, you keep mumbling, and I can't hear you. Speak up."

The man chuckled and grinned. "I mean, if you can't hear me, Your Honor, maybe you need to step away from the bench for a few minutes and go clean your ears."

Some people in the courtroom had the nerve to laugh. I just looked at the poor fool and shook my head. He had no clue how much power the judge had over him. Cooperation was badly needed. Even I knew that.

"Get this idiot out of here," the judge said to the bailiff. "I don't have time for this."

After that, every case he listened to went downhill. Fines were astronomical, he kept cutting people off—it seemed as if he had somewhere else he needed to be.

"Your Honor," a prissy petite woman said, "I was not speeding. The officer who pulled me over was very mean to me, and my three-year-old daughter was in the car as well. She couldn't stop crying because his voice was so loud as he yelled at me."

The officer defended himself as the woman dabbed her teary eyes. Today, the officer seemed very polite. "I never would have yelled had she not cursed at me and threatened to call her husband who's a lawyer. She made ongoing threats about him having the power to have me fired."

The judge put a stop to the madness when he gave the woman a hefty fine for speeding and for not wearing a seat belt. Basically, her tears didn't work. That made me nervous, and when I looked up and saw Brent enter the courtroom with his wife, I became even more nervous. They were holding hands. Both of them had on suits; his was black, hers was navy. She wore it well and her black high heels made her look taller. She looked at me, my hair in particular, and rolled her eyes. I looked rather nice too. The white ruffled blouse I wore, along with my gray pencil skirt, was suitable for the courtroom. I didn't want too many of my curves to show. The more conservative, the better.

"Is Abigail Wilson in the courtroom?"

I quickly stood. "Yes, Your Honor, I'm here."

"Step forward. Do you have an attorney with you?"

"No, sir, I don't. I'm here representing myself."

My legs shook as I stood at the wooden table in front of him. My palms were sweaty, and I took a deep breath because my stomach was starting to hurt. The pain deepened more when he called Brent's name. He was asked the same about an attorney, but Brent replied that he didn't have one either.

"The person I brought with me today is my wife. She's been subjected to some of the terror Miss Wilson has brought our way, and she's my witness."

Yeah, yeah, whatever, I thought, *terror, my ass.* Brent knew better. From the way he had spoken, I could tell he was prepared.

"If I have any questions for your wife," the judge said, "I'll ask her to step forward. Meanwhile, ma'am, please go have a seat in the courtroom."

Ha! I wanted to shout out loudly. She wanted to be by Brent's side, but the judge wasn't having it. He summarized the charges against me and asked for a plea.

"Not guilty, sir. May I please tell you why?"

The judge peered over his glasses, looking at me, and then at Brent. "Okay, folks. What's going on here? You first, Miss Wilson, and please make it brief."

I quickly went into great detail about how Brent had abused me, used me, and refused to let the situation go. My photos backed up everything, especially the photo I had recently taken of him lying on his bed with no clothes on.

"For whatever crazy reason . . ." I said tearfully as the judge flipped through the photos. A frown was on his face. He sighed too. "I still love this man with all of my heart, even though he has done me wrong. I knew that being intimate with him the other day wasn't the right thing to do, but he was so forceful. I just didn't want to fight with him again. I tried not to fight with him, even when he made me cut my hair off so I could look more like his wife."

Brent just couldn't bite his tongue and wait until he was called on to speak. Had he been here earlier, he would have known that the judge was not in the mood for his outburst.

"She's lying!" Brent barked as he looked at me. "I can't believe you're lying like this. Just who are you, Abby, some kind of psychopath?"

The judge's face was twisted as he looked at Brent. "There will be no such talk like that in my courtroom. Do not speak unless I ask you to. And don't you say another word to her."

Brent shook his head in disgust. The judge addressed me again. "Tell me about the school incident. Why were you there?"

"Because Brent had jumped on me the night before. I was so upset after I left the hospital, and I really wanted to do something that would make him stop this. I confronted him at work, but it was never my intentions to scare those children. Brent was the one who started yelling at me, and then he ordered his students out of the classroom. He was the one who scared them, and after they left, he punched . . ." I paused to wipe a tear and swallow the lump in my throat. "He punched me in my face for coming there. But all I wanted to do was talk to him."

"Come on, Abby," Brent shouted. "Quit lying! I did *not* punch you. I have never, *ever* put my hands on you, and you know it!"

The judge responded before I did. "If that's the case, how did she get all of these bruises on her body?"

Brent shrugged and was unable to come up with the right answer. "I . . . I don't know. I guess she put them there herself."

The judge gave him a look that could have shattered him into a thousand pieces. He glanced at the photos again. "Mr. Carson, look at this picture. Tell me if that's you, and tell me when that photo was taken."

The bailiff gave one of the pictures to Brent. I wasn't sure which one it was, but I had an idea.

Brent looked at it and shook his head. "That's me, but I can't recall when the photo was taken."

I willingly helped the judge out. "It was taken last week while I was at his house having sex with him. His wife had left, and he invited me to come over."

"No, *you* were having sex," Brent barked at me again. "I wasn't, and I *never* invited you to come to my house. Your Honor, this . . . This crazy woman broke into my home, came into the bathroom while I was taking a shower, and pretended to be my wife. She put a knife to my neck while she performed oral sex on me."

There were a few gasps in the courtroom, but dead silence as well. Brent didn't know how ridiculous he sounded. I wanted to laugh, but in no way would I halt what was about to go down.

"So, the picture was taken about a week ago?" the judge asked.

"Yes, I believe so, sir. I couldn't stop her from taking it because she had a knife in her hand."

"Did you report the break-in to the police?"

Brent sighed again. "No, sir. I didn't think they would believe me, as you don't seem to right now."

The judge asked Brent's wife to step forward. She had a mean mug on her face. Her eyes stayed focused on the judge. He hit her with a question that she wasn't prepared to answer.

"At any time, did your husband tell you about Miss Wilson breaking into your home, entering the bathroom, and pulling a knife on him?"

She answered with a straight face. "No, he did not."

Boom! I thought. This Negro didn't even tell her.

"I . . . I didn't say anything because she, my wife, has been fearful of this woman. She keeps showing up at our house, following us, making threats—Your Honor, it's been hell."

"The only person going through hell has been me," I said. "I don't want to take up much more of your time, sir, I know you're a very busy man. But Brent Carson wants to have his cake and eat it too. He wants to be with his wife, but he doesn't want to let me go. If he would just let go and leave me alone, he and his wife, I'll be okay. She's blaming all of this on me, and for God's sake, look at what she did to my car."

The judge flipped through the photos, again, looking at the damages to my car.

"Bitch, you are good!" Lajuanna shouted. "I can't even listen to any more of this. Are you done with me, Your Honor?"

"I am now," he said, pointing to the door. "Out! You will not use that type of language in my courtroom."

Bye, Lajuuuuanna. This was hilarious. And after she left, or should I say, was ejected from the courtroom, things got even worse for Brent. The judge had the students' sworn statements about what had actually happened that day. But he was so livid with Brent's behavior that he didn't even question why I wrote what I did on the chalkboard.

"Excuse me, but I lost my job because of her actions! A black man don't get no justice in the white man's courtroom . . . This is flat-out ridiculous! I haven't had an opportunity to tell you all that this woman has been doing to me and my wife."

The judge fired back. "I don't know if she's been doing anything to your wife, but it is quite clear that she has been doing a whole lot of things with you. I've given you ample opportunities to answer my questions, but you seem not to be able to recall certain instances that can help you clear your name. I don't believe for one minute that Miss Wilson has been innocent in all of this, but I do believe that you have put her, as well as your wife, in a position that seems to have everyone at war."

The judge almost had it right. I wanted to clap, but couldn't.

Unfortunately, for him, Brent couldn't control his anger. "No, sir, that is *not* the case! That is *not* the fucking case, and I need you to do something . . . anything to stop this woman who is on the verge of hurting someone or getting hurt her damn self! If you refuse to do anything, I will take matters into my own hands and deal with her myself!"

"Looks to me like you've been doing that all along. Maybe you need to sit in jail for a few days and think about your actions. Think about why this is happening to you and figure out a way to calm yourself down. You—"

Brent cut the judge off as he was speaking. "And maybe all you need to do is just listen. Clean your ears and listen!"

Well, that just about did it. The last thing the judge wanted to hear was another black man telling him to clean out his ears. At the snap of his fingers, he ordered that Brent spend five days in jail.

Brent was seething with anger as two officers pulled his arms behind his back, cuffing him.

I stood, forcing tears to come out of my eyes. It was an Oscar-winning performance, especially when I stretched out my hand to him, expressing how sorry I was. "Please don't be upset with me," I said. "All I want is the best for yoooou."

"Fuck you!" he hissed as they pulled him out of the courtroom. "And this isn't over with, Abby. I can promise you that!"

The judge was disgusted, as was everyone else in the courtroom who looked on in disbelief. He wrapped the case up when he gave me a $500 fine for trespassing on school property. I didn't mind paying the fine. Seeing Brent in handcuffs was certainly enough satisfaction for me.

I left the courtroom on cloud nine. That was . . . until the elevator opened and I felt a tightened fist slam right into my mouth. The punch was so powerful that it knocked me on my ass. I skidded backward, and that was when I saw Lajuanna jump on top of me like a raging tiger. She held my throat while lifting my head and banging it on the ground.

"Bitch, I will kill you, you hear me! If you come to my house again, you are one dead woman!"

I cried out in so much pain. My head was hurting, my brain was rattled.

"Stop it!" I heard a woman yell. "Get your hands off her!"

"Oh my God! She's going to kill her! Somebody, help!"

Lajuanna was a madwoman. She slapped my face, then stood to kick me. I cradled myself on the floor, with my hands over my face, trying to protect it.

"Stop or I'll shoot!" an officer yelled. "Back away from her now!"

Lajuanna was out of breath as she backed away from me. With pride in her eyes, she grinned as she held her hands behind her back, glaring at me.

I sat up, feeling blood stirring in my mouth and with a very sore head.

"How did *that* feel?" she asked as the cop handcuffed her. "And if you want more of that, you know where to find me."

The cop pulled her away, while another one stayed to get a statement from me. There were several witnesses and also onlookers who lined the stairs by the elevators, wondering what in the hell had just happened. I was embarrassed and sore all over. The cop asked if I needed a doctor, but I declined. After he took my statement, I was able to leave. I walked to my car in pain, and unfortunately for me, when I got there, my windshield had been cracked again. I figured Lajuanna must have done it, but she was, undeniably, going to pay for it.

As I sat in my car, I wiped blood from my mouth with tissue I had in the glove compartment. I wiped my face with the tissue too, and then lifted my shirt to see if there were any bruises on my side because it hurt so badly. All

I saw was some of my skin that was raw and bleeding. It had turned red. I predicted that a bruise would appear later—an ugly bruise at that.

I started my car, and before I drove off, I picked up my cell phone to see if Kendal had called me. She hadn't, so I sent her a text message, telling her to come home. She replied by the time I reached the stoplight. Her reply was: No.

I was pissed off. Seeing Brent in handcuffs wasn't enough to calm me. Seeing his wife in handcuffs didn't help either, but maybe something else would. I drove to their house. And using the same key that I never returned to the hidden spot on the porch, I opened the door and went inside, as if I lived there myself.

The first thing I did was find a clean shirt to put on, since mine was bloody. Lajuanna had some nice items hanging in the closet, so I chose a silk green blouse that buttoned down the front. The color is what caught my eyes. So did some of her other clothes. Like a jazzy-orange dress that was pleated at the bottom, a white suit with tiny diamond studs on the cuffs, and a pair of jeans that were pretty darn expensive. I even saw some shoes that I liked. But when I tried them on, her feet were much smaller than mine.

I gathered the items I wanted and laid them in a chair. Afterward, I changed my shirt in the bathroom, and used a clean white cloth to wipe my swollen lip and face. I looked in the mirror with anger in my eyes. My lip was real puffy. That bitch had to pay for this.

As I looked around and opened a few drawers, I found a pair of scissors. I went back into the closet, cutting up her clothes, as well as some of his. It took me awhile, but when all was said and done, the closet was nothing pretty. Shreds of their clothes hung from hangers, and many were cut and thrown on the floor. I swiped my hands together.

"Looks good to me," I said and turned my attention to their messy bed.

The stains let me know that they'd probably had sex this morning. Brent was such a damn horny dog. I couldn't help but to laugh when I'd thought about his performance at the courthouse. It was stupid of him not to tell his wife I had been here. The look on both of their faces was priceless. Nevertheless, no lawyer was needed and the verdict was in. Both of them were in jail—right where they belong.

And since they wouldn't be coming home soon, I continued to make a disaster of the place. I used the scissors in my hand to cut their sheets.

I stabbed the mattress and sliced the pillows. Feathers rained everywhere, all over me, as well as on the floor. Almost satisfied with my work, I swayed my hand across their dresser, making everything on top hit the floor. Several bottles of their fragrances cracked open and spilled. It was a little mess, but certainly not enough.

"*Ding, ding,*" I said as a little bell went off in my head. "Now, *that's* a good idea." I went to both bathrooms, turning on the water to fill the tub. As water filled in the second tub, I gazed at it with a glass of wine in one hand, a cigarette in the other. Brent always had the good stuff, and red wine was his favorite. I drank a little, and then poured the rest in the tub. I put the glass in my purse, and as water started to spill over the tub and flood the floor, I laughed. I took several more puffs from the cigarette, and before things got too messy, I locked the door on my way out, just in case somebody tried to break in.

For real, this time, I was finally pleased.

Chapter Eleven

I hadn't heard from Brent or his wife for almost two weeks now. Hadn't heard much from Kendal either. It was obvious that she didn't want to be here with me. I begged her to come home so we could talk, but she felt as if she was grown and talking to her mother was beneath her. Sometimes, lessons had to be learned. Kendal was going to get a big lesson behind this. I let her stay right where she wanted, for now, but, sooner or later, she would have to deal with me.

Meanwhile, I had gotten my car windshield fixed, again, and it was back to work for me. I didn't have much time off left, and trust me when I say, I hated to return to work. The second I arrived, I was asked by upper management to go see Mrs. Thiele. She was an old, Goody Two-shoes trick who I couldn't stand. She acted as if she owned the place, and she was always looking at me with jealousy in her eyes.

"Have a seat, Abigail," she said. "I'm glad you're back because I need to discuss some things with you."

I wasn't sure what she wanted to discuss until she started talking about a report that I had been stealing from the store and selling merchandise on the streets. She claimed to have evidence. When I asked to see it, she refused to show it to me.

"Not only that, but we've had numerous complaints about your behavior. Several customers called and spoke about how nasty you were toward them. I don't know what's going on with you, but this is unacceptable. We won't be pressing charges against you for the merchandise, but we've decided to terminate your employment with us, effective immediately."

My mouth was wide open. "Are you serious? I've been here for years, Mrs. Thiele. Not once have I taken anything, and I've always worked my ass off. That's why, when the management position became available, I had no problem getting the job. I've never had any complaints, and if I wanted to steal clothes from here, I would have done it a long time ago. I've been on vacation for a few weeks, so how can someone complain about me when I haven't even been here?"

"They did complain, and they've been complaining for a long time. Now, I've said all there is to say about this, and I will say no more. Other than thanks for your service and good-bye, Ms. Wilson. Good luck."

I wanted to jump over the desk and beat her ass! Instead, I stood, held my head up high, and tucked my purse underneath my arm.

"Good luck to you too, Mrs. Thiele. May you go straight to hell, old bitch."

Her mouth dropped opened as I walked out. I figured she would do everything in her power to hold my final check. If she did, that would mean trouble for her.

Sickened by being fired, I drove home in a daze. Things seemed to be falling apart, and, yes, I knew karma was a bitch. No question, I had done some dirty mess. But Brent pushed me to the edge like no one had ever done before. It was the only way for me to get him back. I was done with him, but that didn't stop me from driving by his house to see what was up. This time, however, his house looked different. There were no curtains or blinds covering the windows. No cars were in the driveway, and mail was sticking out of the mailbox. The plants on the porch were gone, grass was a little high, and the house, basically, looked deserted. I parked my car, and when I went to a window to look inside, it was empty. Every last piece of furniture was gone. They had moved. I wondered where to. Had he moved out of town or was he still in St. Louis? I surely wanted to know, and since it was Monday, I intended to drop by the pool hall tonight to see if he would be there.

For now, though, my new job search was on. I had some money saved up, but not enough where I could just sit at home and do nothing. I updated my résumé and printed a few copies. I then searched the Internet for job sites that allowed me to upload my résumé and send it right to the company I was interested in. My management status opened the door to many opportunities. I expected to hear back from someone soon.

Around one o'clock, I started to feel hungry. A salad from Arby's sounded good, so I reached for my purse and keys so I could go. I locked my door, then got in my car, cranking up the music. But just as I was almost a mile down the street, I heard a gulping sound that made me lower the volume. I looked on the floor as well as on my seats. The sound continued, and when I glanced in my rearview mirror, I saw what looked to be some type of iguana with green, scaly skin and beady eyes looking right at me. It wasn't small either; I didn't know if it was going to jump on me or not. I slammed my car in park, rushing out as quickly as I could. The iguana turned his head and started snaking his tongue in and out of his mouth. He used his claws to move from one side of my car to the other. My flesh crawled. I hated animals like this. I damn near wanted to run, but I had to get him out of my car. Nobody whatsoever was around. Not even the person who had put the thing there. I was forced to open the back doors to my car and deal with it.

"Out," I said, shooing it away with my purse. "Get out and go somewhere else."

The damn thing kept looking at me and didn't move. His long tail did, however, but those beady eyes had a lock on me.

"Damn it," I said, looking around. I saw a young white boy coming down the street on a hoverboard. I waved my hands in the air to get his attention. "Excuse me. Can you please come over here and help me?"

He rolled right up to me, and then jumped off the board. "What's up?"

"Do you see that thing in my car? Can you please remove it for me? It's pretty scary to me."

He looked inside the car, and his eyes grew wide as saucers. "Oh my God. That thing is a beauty. How did it get in your car?"

I had an idea, but now wasn't the time to say it. "I don't know. I just opened my door, and there it was."

"That's pretty cool, man. It's an iguana. You don't see many of those around here, unless someone has it as a pet."

The last thing I wanted was an educational lesson on iguanas. The look I gave the young man implied just that. He reached in the car, carefully picked it up, and laid it across the palm of his hand.

"Hi there, little one," he said, talking to it as if it were a baby. This was crazy. I couldn't believe how unafraid the boy was.

"I'll take him to my house and call animal control. I may ask around too, to see if anyone is missing a pet."

"Thank you so much." I reached into my purse to give him some money. I touched a fifty-dollar bill, but considering I was out of a job, I reached for a twenty. "Here you go. I hope you find a home for that thing. Good luck."

He smiled and took the money from my hand. As the iguana rested on his arm, the boy rolled off on the hoverboard again. I shook my head, already suspecting who had put that in my car. It was either Brent or his wife. If they wanted to keep this up, so be it. I just needed to find out where they lived and find out fast.

After the ordeal with the iguana was over, I got my salad and returned home. This time, someone had sprayed red paint on my white garage doors. The letters WHORE were scripted on it, and just so no one would see it, I rushed out of my car and raised my garage door. Unlike Brent and his wife, I wasted no time calling the police to report the incident. An officer was there within ten minutes. And, to my surprise, it was Officer Wayne. The same officer I had spoken to at the station, on Kendal's birthday.

"Good afternoon," he said, removing his dark sunglasses that shielded his hooded eyes.

He was so sexy to me—his uniform was a perfect fit for his muscular frame. Right about now, I could have taken him into my house and screwed his brains out, just to release some of my tension.

"What seems to be the problem here?"

I sighed. "Unfortunately, I think my ex-boyfriend is at it again. We went to court a few weeks ago, and he was given jail time for his behavior. I'm sure he's upset, and that's why he did this to my garage. He also put an iguana in my car this morning. I almost died, and thankfully, one of the kids around here removed it for me."

I lowered the garage to show him what I was talking about. He shook his head. "Why don't

you get a restraining order against this man?
You really need to start there and have him
served."

"Served where? He moved. I don't know where
he lives, and that benefits him." I started to get
emotional. Just wanted a little comfort right
now.

He appeared very sympathetic. "Everything
will be okay. What did you say the gentleman's
name was?" He removed a notepad from his
pocket, as well as a pen. When his pen didn't
work, he asked if I had one he could use.

"Yes, I do. It's inside. You can follow me."

I purposely swayed my hips from side to side,
making sure he got a glimpse of my booty. After
we went inside, I opened a drawer in the kitchen,
pulling out a pen.

"Here you go," I said, handing it to him.
"His name is Brent Carson. His wife's name is
Lajuanna Carson. She's involved in the harassment too. And she was arrested as well for jump-
ing on me at the courthouse."

I told him most of what had happened since
I'd left the police station that day. I even mentioned how everything had gone in court. He was
very much tuned in, especially when I answered
my phone and no one said anything.

"See? This is the kind of stuff that just keeps on happening. I feel so trapped by Brent. I live here alone, and I'm so afraid that he's going to come here and do something to me."

"Just because he moved, it doesn't mean he can't be found. I'll see what I can find out. Meanwhile, go get that restraining order. I'll also drive by every now and then, just to make sure everything is okay. My name is Eric. Don't be alarmed when you see my car outside. I just want to keep my eyes on things."

"Thank you so much. I will feel much safer. And if there is anything that I can do for you . . . any more information I can provide, please let me know."

His eyes shifted to my breasts, and then to my face. "I'll let you know," he said, before turning to leave.

I just wanted to squeeze my hands on his nice ass and take him to my bedroom. Time and patience, though, were very much needed.

After he left, I went to Home Depot to get some white paint for my garage. Clinton was on my mind, so I drove to his apartment to see if he would paint the garage for me, so I didn't have to. Like clockwork, he was outside. He did a lot of hanging around, doing nothing. I guessed with a woman like Velma, what other choice did he have?

I parked my car, but before I got out, he came up to it. He didn't look excited to see me. I assumed he was unhappy about me not picking him up that Saturday.

"I wish that when you say you gon' doing something, that you would stop tripping and just do it. I had my hopes up, and I was damn sure looking forward to making some extra money."

"Get in the car and stop griping," I said. "You're starting to sound like Velma. I have a good explanation, if you want to hear it."

Clinton got in the car to hear me out.

"I lost my job, okay? Had to deal with my ex in court and my daughter ran away from home. There's been a lot going on. The last thing I needed to think about was getting my basement fixed up. I'm sorry about the money thing, but at this point, I'm not really sure if I will have anything extra to get my basement done. I do, however, have a small project that you can do to earn fifty bucks. Somebody spray painted the word *whore* on my garage. It needs to be painted, so if you could do that for me, I really would appreciate it."

There was a toothpick in his mouth. He pulled it out and nodded his head. "I can do that, but I warned you about that ex of yours. That cat's crazy."

"Yes, he is. He and his wife. I'm sure she's the one who did it."

"Maybe so, but don't let him off the hook. He probably put her up to it. Regardless, when do you want it taken care of?"

"Like right now. I can't leave my garage down with that word on it. In any neighborhood, especially mine, something like that is pretty embarrassing."

"I'm sure it is. And I apologize for the way I acted. It's just that I thought I'd make some good money on a project like framing your basement. I kind of got my hopes up real high."

"I understand. I'm sorry, and I'll ask around to see if some of my friends need something done."

"Cool," he said. "I'll be right back. Need to go upstairs and tell Velma where I'm going. What time do you think we'll be back?"

"Probably within a few hours or so. I'm not sure."

Clinton got out of the car, returning five minutes later. "She good," he said. "Let's go."

I doubted that she was good. She probably wasn't there. If she was, I'm sure he wouldn't have made it back so quickly.

Within the hour, we were back at my place. Clinton had on the nice T-shirt I had bought him and a pair of jeans. I didn't want him to get any paint on his clothes, so I gave him a clear trash bag to cover up with. He laughed.

"I'm good, Mama. Save the bags for trash. I promise not to drip any paint on me."

I laid the plastic bag on the ground and let him get to work. He asked if I had a way to play some music, so I turned up the volume on a tiny radio in the garage so he could listen. He bobbed his head to the rap music, and as I watched him carefully paint the door, I thought about asking Clinton to kill Brent for me. For the right amount of money, I was sure he would do it. I just didn't know how to get my hands on a large sum of cash. Until I did, I squashed those thoughts, saving them for another day.

In less than an hour, Clinton was finished. WHORE was gone, and there was no trace of it. We started to clean up the minimal mess he'd made. And when I looked up, I saw Officer Wayne slowly roll by in his car. He nodded, and I waved. Clinton looked at him, then at me.

"I see they're awfully friendly around here. In my hood, it ain't going down like that."

"He's one of the nice ones. The others are not like him, trust me."

They surely weren't sexy like him either. Unfortunately, I saw the wedding ring on his finger. However, there was a chance that I would work around it.

After Clinton and I cleaned up, I offered to make him dinner. I had been lonely since Kendal wasn't here. I needed someone to talk to, more so, someone I didn't have to argue with. Clinton agreed to stay. He actually helped me cook, and as we sat at the table to eat the baked chicken and mashed potatoes, he inquired about Kendal.

"Do you know where she's at?"

"I do. She's at a friend's house. I've tried to get her to come home, but she refuses to."

"How can she refuse anything when you're the adult and she's the child?"

"I know that, but I don't want to make matters worse than what they already are."

Clinton looked at me with seriousness in his eyes. "Never forget who's in charge. Pushing shit under the rug doesn't help, and believe me when I say your daughter needs you."

"Well, she acts like she doesn't. She said it herself that she no longer wants to live here. I've done everything for her, and as long as I'm doing something nice, it's all good."

"You may have done things for her, but have you been her mother? She needs guidance, nurturing, love and respect. She also needs your time. How much time do the two of you spend together?"

"Enough. She doesn't like being around me, and every chance she gets, she's always running to her friends. She's a teenager. This phase will be over with soon enough. At least, I hope it will."

"There's a reason why she's always running, teenager or not. I'm not judging you, but it sounds like the two of you have some work to do."

I had to go there, even though I didn't want to. But when hypocrisy was the name of the game, I had to call a person out on it.

"We may have work to do, but so do you and your son, Clinton. His 'crazy' mother can't be your excuse for not seeing him, and if it is, then that's on you."

Clinton chewed his food and nodded. "I'm not in denial. I know I have major work to do. My son hasn't been in my life for a long time, but we have been making a little progress. I'm just trying to spare you some of the pain I've felt over the years. Realize your mistakes and make the relationship between you and your daughter better."

Maybe I had been a little stubborn about the situation. Clinton's words caused me to open my eyes a little. I appreciated his company more than he knew, and when the time came for us to go, I let him know how I felt.

"Before we leave," I said, standing in the foyer in front of him, "thanks for the advice earlier. I'll go find Kendal tomorrow and make her talk to me."

"That's right. Put your foot down and stop being passive. You have to be a little more aggressive, especially when you want to accomplish something."

He said it, I didn't. Being aggressive paid off. I told him that I needed to go get something from my bedroom, but instead of retrieving something, I hurried to remove my clothes. I sprayed my entire body with dashes of sweet perfume, and then I paraded down the hallway in nothing but my skin. Clinton was still by the door waiting for me. When I called his name, he turned around. His eyes zoomed in, scanning me like a laser.

"You said be aggressive," I said, halting my steps in front of him. I lifted his hand, placing it on my breast. "Is this being too aggressive?"

His hand didn't move. He held it there, and when I lifted his other hand, he pulled both hands back.

"Listen, Abby, you are probably one of the sexiest women I've ever had in my presence, but you know I can't do this and why."

I silenced the noise when I leaned in to kiss him. He finally reciprocated, his hand slowly traveled to my ass, squeezing it.

"See," I said between kisses, "is this so hard? Isn't it easy to do this?"

As close as I was to Clinton, I could feel his dick rise against me. My pussy was tingling; I was *so* ready to feel what I had seen the other day inside of me. I could tell he would be good. Something inside told me he was, but my thoughts were cut short when he backed away from me. He scratched his head while licking his lips and looking at my breasts again.

"Sorry, Mama, this ain't happening. I got a girl at the crib who I adore. She may not be perfect, but I can't cheat on her. Especially not when she's pregnant. If we ever depart ways for good, I promise to come back here and hook us both up."

I was in total disbelief that he had turned me down. My feelings were bruised. I continued to try to persuade him. "I am *soooo* horny, Clinton, and I . . . I've been thinking about being with you a lot. Have you even thought about having sex with me?"

"Of course I have. All the time, and it makes me feel hella guilty. Velma knows I've been thinking about it too. And just the other day, I called her your name by accident. Regardless,

I don't want to hurt her. She may not be good enough in your eyes, but she is in mine."

I was so stunned by his devotion to her. What in the hell was wrong with him?

"I don't believe your dedication to her. There's something more to it. Tell me, Clinton, please. I need to know why you really don't want to have sex with me."

He stood in thought for a few seconds, looked at the floor, then scanned my body again. "I just don't want to hurt you. I don't want you involved in what I'm going through with Velma, and I'm asking that you respect that."

I ignored what he'd said and reached for his hand again. This time, I made him feel how wet my insides were. He lightly rubbed his fingers inside of me and closed his eyes. "Man, you tripping," he said. "Do you have any condoms around here?"

"I don't think so, but let's stop and get some for next time. For now, I need this."

I reached for Clinton's zipper to unzip his jeans. His dick was hard, long, and growing. It drew me right in. But as soon as I touched it, he backed away and removed his fingers from my insides.

"Let's go," he said. "Please, let's go. I can't and I won't do this. It's not right."

I wasn't about to beg him for sex. This was so ridiculous, and instead of continuing to make a fool of myself, I returned to my room to put on my clothes. When I came back, Clinton was still waiting on me. He walked up and gave me a kiss on the cheek.

"Stay sexy, all right? And if you feel as if we can't be friends, don't bother to pick me up again."

I swear my face had cracked and hit the floor. Rejection didn't feel good. I held a smile on my face, though, but deep inside, I was crushed.

I opened the door so we could leave. And as soon as I backed out of the driveway, I saw a police car again. I wasn't sure who was inside because it was too dark. My gut, however, told me it was Officer Wayne.

"Damn, they don't play around here, do they?" Clinton said. "All they do is case the streets all day long."

"Lately, more than usual," I said. "But that's a good thing, especially in my case where I have a crazy ex."

"You keep saying that, but it doesn't seem as if you're doing much to get him off your back. I mean, if it were me, I would knock a mutha off for harassing me like that."

"I wish I had the guts to do it. I even thought about paying someone to do it for me. But I only have about six or seven thousand in the bank. I'm sure someone would want much more than that to get rid of Brent for good for me."

Clinton was quiet, as if he was in deep thought. He finally spoke up and responded to my comment. "I would do it for five, but too bad I don't get down like that anymore. I have a baby on the way, my son and I are trying to patch things up, and you already know how I feel about Velma. She would be devastated if I agreed to do some shit like that and got caught. That's what I fear the most. And going back to jail ain't an option."

"Oh, I wouldn't want you to. I wasn't thinking about asking you to do it. I was just speaking in general about how much someone would probably want me to pay them. That's all."

"Aw, okay. But if you really want to get that done, let me know. I know some brothers who will knock him off for five or six hundred dollars. All you have to do is say the word and I'll put you in touch with them."

I cocked my head back and took my eyes off the road to look at him. "Are you serious? For five or six hundred bucks? That's crazy."

"Woman, please. Where have you been living? These mofos out here killing folks for twenty dollars. It's all about the money. Money can get you just about anything your heart desires, including a dead ex."

I remained quiet and was in deep thought about what I wanted to happen to Brent. Clinton didn't say much else either. Considering what had happened at my house earlier, and our conversation in the car, I had a good ole feeling that this was going to be my last trip to his place. I parked my car in front of his apartment building. Wanting to pay him for painting my garage, I reached in my purse to give him the fifty dollars.

"Thanks again," I said, handing the money over to him. "If I can think of anything else I need you to do, I'll be in touch."

"You're welcome. And don't forget what I told you about your daughter, Abby. When all is said and done, she is more worth it than your ex is."

"I know. And don't you forget what I said to you about your son."

"Fair enough."

He opened the door and got out. I didn't bother to wait like I normally did. I just drove off. But almost five blocks from his place, I could see a car speeding up from behind me. The lights started flashing. At first, I thought it was a police car. I pulled over, and when it swerved around me, I saw Velma driving. She parked in front of my car, cutting me off. And when she got out of the car, I didn't dare lower my window. She pounded her fist against it.

"Bitch, I know you've been fucking my man! Why are you screwing him when you know I'm pregnant by him? I will kill you, ho. You need to leave him the hell alone!"

I just couldn't let this foolishness continue. As far as I knew, Clinton seemed to be a decent man. Why was she so insecure? What had he done to make her act this way? He damn sure was no Brent. I only wished that he had been as up front with me as Clinton was. And no matter what anybody thought, I had every reason to conduct myself the way I did. At least, that was what I'd told myself.

I lowered my window, firing back at Velma. "I don't know what is wrong with you, but I am *not* screwing your man. He is completely loyal to you, so what in the hell is your problem?"

"Loyal? Bitch, please. You ain't loyal, and neither is he. If he was, I wouldn't have found a pair of women's panties in his pocket. I wouldn't have seen a used condom in his dirty clothes, he wouldn't have given me a STD, and another bitch wouldn't be pregnant with his baby. Where is the loyalty in that shit? Huh?"

Ooops, maybe I had gotten it wrong. There had to be a *real* reason for her behavior, and if everything she said was true, I definitely didn't have an answer for her. All I could do was defend myself so I could get away from this crazy heifer.

"I'm not the one, Velma. Clinton and I have never had sex. I promise you that all he's done is work on a few jobs for me. That's it."

She put her hand on her hip while mean mugging me. "Have you kissed him? Go ahead and lie, bitch, because I saw y'all kissing in yo' car. That's why I hope you like the new decorations on your garage. I hope you liked my pet too, and for the record, I know where you work, where you live—everything! I've seen you in action, Miss Stalker. But guess what? The stalker done got stalked! By *me,* and you didn't even know it. Now that you know, do me one favor. I asked once, I'll ask again. Don't bring yo' ass back here ever again!"

She had my full attention after that. I couldn't believe she was responsible for what had been going on, and if she was the one who had gotten me fired from my job, I was about to let this bitch have it. I pushed on the door, but she pushed it back toward me. And when I attempted to push it again, that's when she pulled out a gun that was tucked behind her.

"Get outta that car and I'll make you regret it! Leave and don't come back! If you and Clinton want to do something behind my back, the two of you will pay for it! I'm sick and tired of being fucked over! This is the last damn straw!"

She started to sob with the gun trembling in her hand. And as tears poured down her face, dripping from her chin, I felt Velma's pain. I was tired too. Clinton straight-up had me convinced that he was one of the good guys. Brent had convinced me of the same thing. They both were low down. I hoped that Velma gave him exactly what he deserved. She was just barking up the wrong tree when it came to me.

"Please go take this up with Clinton and move your car so I can get out of here. Lower the gun too. It's not even necessary because, for the last time, he and I have never had sex."

She nodded her head. "Y'all would have, especially if he had given in to your advances tonight. And the only reason he hasn't is because that nigga is HIV positive! I guess he wanted to spare you the trouble. He damn sure didn't spare my ass or his other baby's mama!"

My heart fell straight to my stomach. I could have died! I didn't know if Velma was lying or not, but what she said could've very well been true. And as I thought about it more . . . his words, his actions, his blatant rejection . . . It all made sense. He wasn't in love. That fool had HIV! I was so glad that tonight turned out as it had.

Velma gripped the gun tighter. I wasn't sure what she was going to do, so I quickly swerved my car to the left, knocking her back several feet. She hit the ground hard, and when I looked in my rearview mirror, she was rocking back and forth in the street. I didn't know what to do. I was sure that someone was probably looking out of their window and had seen what had happened. Hopefully, they called an ambulance for her. Soon, because, as I glanced in my rearview mirror, it looked as if she had stopped moving.

Chapter Twelve

For the next few days, I stayed tuned in to the news to see if anything had been reported about a hit-and-run. I saw nothing on TV, nor did I see anything in the newspaper or on the Internet when I checked. I was worried about Velma. She didn't deserve any of this. If what she'd said about Clinton was true, I hope she killed him. I wanted to drive to their apartment to find out what had happened, but I decided to stay as far away from there as possible. If anything severe had happened, and someone knew that I was responsible, I was sure the cops would come looking for me. Until then, I focused on finding a job and on trying to repair my relationship with Kendal. It had been too long since I had seen her, and it was as if she had no desire to see me.

I did, however, take Clinton's advice. I found out where Tammi and her mother had moved to simply by looking up her name on the Internet.

I typed in Brent's info too, but nothing came up. He'd just vanished—I still wondered where he was. Too much had happened on Monday night. I didn't have time to go to the pool hall or bowling alley. Maybe I would go this Monday, just to make sure everything was good with him and his wife.

While waiting at the end of the street, I saw Barbara pull her car into a parking spot. The apartment complex they lived in was just okay, and with only two bedrooms, I figured things were pretty cramped. Tammi was in the front seat of the car, Kendal was in the back. Tammi and her mother got out first, and when Kendal got out, I almost couldn't believe my eyes. She had picked up weight. Her belly had a serious bulge in it. It wasn't until she turned sideways when I finally saw for myself that she was pregnant. I covered my mouth, damn near wanting to cry. I couldn't, because anger crept up on me so fast that I pressed on the accelerator, driving my car so fast that they all turned their heads. I hopped out of the car, looking at Kendal who had wide eyes.

"Now I see why you didn't want to come home." I slammed my car door shut, marching up to her. "Why didn't you tell me you were pregnant? Is this why you don't want to come home?"

With much attitude on display, she folded her arms. "Because you wouldn't have cared if I told you or not."

I raised my hand, almost slapping the shit out of her for getting smart with me. Barbara, however, grabbed my hand.

"No, Abby. The last thing she needs is for you to come over here, smacking her around. Are you ready to come inside so we can talk?"

"I can talk to my daughter alone. You people have already interfered enough!"

"I don't want to talk to you," Kendal said. "I have nothing to say, other than good-bye."

She turned to walk away from me. I reached out and grabbed her arm, squeezing it as tight as I could.

"My patience is wearing thin with you, young lady. Tighten your lips before I smack you in your mouth!"

"Go right ahead," she said, snatching away from me. "Violence is all you know. It's your answer to everything, and I hope that works out for you."

Kendal walked away again. This time, I didn't stop her. I was embarrassed by the way she treated me. She had been brainwashed. These people had brainwashed my child. I was damn mad about it too.

Barbara stepped in front of me, trying to be the voice of reason. "Give her more time," she said. "I know this isn't easy, but she's really going through a lot. Maybe you and I can—"

I held my hand up to stop her from talking. Somebody was responsible for this, and I wasn't going to take all of the blame. "Barbara, you have nothing to say to me. You should have told me that she was pregnant. If it was your child, I would've called to discuss everything with you. But the truth is, you love every bit of this. You and Tammi have always been jealous of us. This is what you had hoped for, and since you want to replace me, go right ahead. Do your best with Kendal and good luck to you both!"

I stormed off with tears in my eyes. I guess the advice Clinton told me was no good after all. I shouldn't have listened. Because at the end of the day, Kendal wanted to be in control, and I intended to let her. That's what I kept telling myself, but I had gotten to the point where I needed some serious help with her. I couldn't do this alone. Malik needed to step in and do something quickly.

Instead of going home, I found myself parked outside of his house. I stayed in the car for a while, wondering if this was, indeed, the right thing to do. Thus far, he hadn't stepped up to provide much help. But now that Kendal was pregnant, maybe he would be willing to talk to her or do something that could help to ease this situation a little. I didn't have any other place to turn. The least I could do was try.

I got out of my car and went to the door. The two-story house Malik lived in was pretty decent. I had no complaints. I figured his drug money helped pay for it, but the way he'd been gambling, he was sure to lose it all. I rang the doorbell, and a few minutes later, the chick I had seen him with at Soulard opened the door. She put her hand on her hip and pursed her lips to let me know that I wasn't supposed to be there.

"I didn't come here to speak to you, so relax," I said. "I came to speak to Malik about something real important. Is he here?"

"Yeah, he here, but I don't know if he want to talk to you. You're always so bitter and angry. He be trying to reach out to you, but you always got an attitude."

I hated for a bitch to interfere in matters like this. She didn't even know what she was talking about. She had no clue what Malik and I had been through, so it was wise for her to keep her mouth shut. That's what I wanted to say, but since I was so desperate to speak to Malik, I kept my cool.

"I apologize for coming off that way, but Malik and I have a bad history together that makes me angry at times. Nonetheless, I need to speak to him about our daughter. She's in trouble, and I could really use his help."

I guess those were the magic words, because the chick stepped aside and allowed me to come in. Almost immediately, the strong scent of marijuana hit me. I could hear reggae music playing lightly in the background. I wasn't sure where Malik was, but his companion invited me into the living room to have a seat. I walked into the room, taking a seat on the microfiber red sofa that was just okay. The entire room was too colorful for my taste, and the décor was real busy. I guess the theme was supposed to be African, but with so many whatnots here and there, I wasn't sure where Malik was going with this. Never in a million years would I allow him to do our home like this. He needed a professional decorator bad.

Minutes later, I heard the music go silent. I could hear Malik's footsteps heading my way, and when he entered the living room, a joint was in his hand.

"I can't believe this shit right here," he said. "Let me pinch you, woman, to make sure it's really you."

He walked closer, and as he reached out to touch me, I backed away from him. "Look, Malik. You're high, and I really need for you to get serious with me right now. We have a problem. Kendal is going through some things, and I don't really know how to help her."

He appeared concerned, and when he sat down on the couch next to me, he laid the joint in an ashtray. "Help her with what? To me, the problem is you've been helping her too much. Kendal is spoiled, and she doesn't know how to accept no. I don't mind telling her that, but you, on the other hand, want to give her everything she wants."

"I give her what I can afford. And the problem is, you always tell her no. You don't call to check on her, and every time she asks you for something, the answer is no. For once, can you say yes? Yes, you'll help us get through this?"

"Get through what? What's this all about?"

"Kendal left home a few weeks ago. She's staying with Tammi and her mother. I stopped by there today to talk to Kendal, but the conversation turned ugly. She's pregnant, Malik. I don't know by who, how far along she is, how or when it happened, but your daughter is pregnant."

Malik took a deep breath, then released it. "Well, we damn sure know how it happened. I'm surprised to hear this because Kendal seems like a girl who ain't interested in doing that."

I had to snap back. "How would you know? You're barely around, Malik, and that's why she's seeking relationships with boys who probably don't even give a damn about her."

"Listen," Malik said as his tone increased, "if you came here to blame me for this shit, you can walk yo' ass right back out that door and forget about this. I have nothing to do with Kendal getting pregnant. That's on her, as well as on you. You should have been paying attention to her. You should have taught her better. You should have told her to keep her fucking legs closed, and you should have known the nigga she got pregnant by. Sounds to me like you didn't know shit."

His words caused my anger to boil over. You, you, you! Well, what about *his* ass? He needed to take some responsibility for this too.

"Malik, it must feel good to sit there and blame me for everything, and when you get done pointing your finger, I need your help. Please call your daughter and talk to her. Go see her and ask what you can do to make her come back home. She needs to know that we're both on her side, and maybe if you'll talk to her, she'll listen."

Malik threw his hand back, brushing off my suggestion. "Talk to her? It's too late to talk to her if she's already pregnant. You should have talked to her. Didn't you teach her about the birds and the bees? I don't know what you want me to do. Talking didn't help us, and it damn sure won't help her."

I wanted to take my fist and light his ass up. I couldn't believe how he sat there, as if he just didn't give a damn. I just told him his daughter was pregnant. Wasn't there anything inside of him that wanted to know what he could do to help? I guess not.

"For the last time, Malik, I need you. You know I wouldn't have come here, unless this was real important to me. We're going to lose Kendal. And what about our grandbaby? Won't you be happy to be a grandfather?"

"Hell fucking no," he said bluntly. "I'm too young to be a grandfather. If I talk to Kendal, the only thing I'm going to encourage her to do is have an abortion. She don't need no damn baby. She don't even have a job to help take care of one. You need to be telling her the same thing, and why in the world would you want her to bring a child into this world, when she's a child herself? That's fucked up, Abby. Real fucked up."

I stood with so much anger displayed on my face. My finger pointed in Malik's direction. "The only thing fucked up is you. Those drugs have fried your damn brain, because you're not making any sense. I have truly wasted my time coming here. I'll deal with this on my own, and meanwhile, may you die soon and rot in hell!"

Malik shooed me away with his hand. "Bye, bitch. Save the drama for your other man. Get out of here, now."

I was taken aback by him calling me a bitch. Malik and I used to have some brutal arguments, and every time he went there, he knew that meant trouble. I picked up a pillow from that tacky-ass sofa, and pounded it against his head. It was the only thing I could find, and he'd better be grateful that nothing else hard was within my sights.

"I got your bitch," I said, striking him over and over again with the pillow. He was crouched down, trying to protect his face. "Here it is! Here all of it is! Take that, you useless piece of shit!"

"Pu . . . Put the damn pillow down before you bust it! And get out of here, Abby, before I hurt you!"

I paid him no mind. I was getting it in for all of his ongoing neglect. It felt good to do this, but when I heard a gun click, I quickly turned around.

"He said leave," his girlfriend shouted with a gun in her hand. "If you hit him again, I'm going to use this. And after you're gone, I'm going to dig a nice little grave for you in the backyard. That way, no one will find you."

Now, any other time, a person with a gun aimed at me would have me frightened. But this chick knew better. She simply knew better, and as far as I was concerned, she may as well start digging my grave. I struck Malik in the face again. And after I hit him, I charged at her with the same pillow. Hit her so hard that the gun dropped from her hand and hit the floor.

This time, Malik scrambled to pick it up, and then he grabbed my arm. "You have lost your damn mind! I use to think yo' ass was crazy before, but you have really lost it. Don't you ever come back here again, and as far as Kendal is concerned, she's on her own. She made a decision to open her legs, and she can deal with it. I'm done with both of you."

Malik pulled me toward the door. I scratched at his hands, spit in his face, kicked his legs . . . did everything that I could to pay him back for everything he'd done. None of it seemed to bother him, and after he shoved me on the porch, he slammed the door shut.

"If you don't leave, I'm going to call the police and have you arrested. I'm sure you don't want that, do you?"

"With all those drugs up in there, I'm sure you wouldn't want the cops over here either. But call them, Malik. If that's what you want to do, call them! I'll wait!"

I stomped back to my car, waiting for at least fifteen minutes to see if the cops showed up. Malik was a fool, but he wasn't a damn fool. He knew he wasn't going to call the cops. Because, if he did, I would have him arrested; arrested for not making his child support payments, and for being thousands of dollars in arrears. When I thought about that, I realized what a big mistake it was for me to come here.

Later that night, I tossed and turned in my sleep, thinking about my horrific day. The news was on in the background, and when I heard the name Clinton Jackson, I thought I was dreaming. I jumped from my sleep and quickly sat up. The volume was too low, so I grabbed the remote from the nightstand, hurrying to turn it up.

"We'll have more on this story within the next hour," the reporter said.

I wanted to know now, so I hit the rewind button, causing the TV to go back to the beginning of the report. Many police officers were on the outside of Clinton's apartment. Crime scene tape surrounded the front of the building. A body was being carried out in a body bag, while people in the neighborhood looked on.

"A thirty-six-year-old man and his wife were found dead in their apartment today. It appears to be an apparent murder-suicide, where the woman pulled a gun on her husband, killing him before taking her own life. According to the neighbors, the couple had been very violent with each other. The police had been dispatched to the apartment several times, because the wife accused her husband, Clinton Jackson, of abuse. We'll have more on this story within the next hour."

I sat on the bed stunned. This was so horrific and was too close to home. I felt bad for them both, but if Clinton was the man Velma told me he was, it was just a matter of time when things would explode. At least I knew that I hadn't injured her in a major way that day. Then again, my actions could have sparked some of this. I probably pushed her over the edge. She had definitely had enough. I only wished that I could push Lajuanna over the edge. Brent was the one who needed to be dealt with. She needed to put a bullet in him too, but I guess that little task would be left up to me.

Over the weekend, I hadn't done much. I was kind of numb from what had happened, and every time I looked in my closet or at my garage doors, all I thought about was Clinton. I also couldn't help but to think if he was really HIV positive. What if he and I had had sex? I damn sure didn't have any condoms handy. Brent and I never used them. I guessed that sometimes when things didn't happen, we could only wonder why and just go with the flow. I was trying, but in my case, that was still very difficult for me to do. I needed help, though, help finding out where Brent was. He wasn't going to get his happily-ever-after, especially, since I didn't get mine.

Just as I thought things were no longer looking up, there was a little hope. And one thing that I was sure would happen was Officer Eric Wayne and I would be getting it on real soon. I'd seen him casing the streets around here quite often. Sometimes, I went outside with a little bit of nothing on, just to get his attention. He always nodded; I waved. Today, however, when I was outside in a see-through pajama top and some very short shorts, he parked his car and got out. He walked up the driveway as I was bent over, picking up some tree branches that had fallen from the storm the other day. He removed his cap, holding it in his hand. Waves were flowing on his head for days.

"How's everything been going?" he asked while looking at me behind his dark shades. "Any problems lately?"

"No, not really. I haven't heard anything from my ex, and that's a good thing. I may get a hang-up call every now and then, but for the most part, I think he has moved on. Then again, that may be wishful thinking."

Since the calls had stopped and Velma admitted to doing what she did, I had no worries. Brent and Lajuanna were off the hook. Officer Wayne didn't have to know that, though.

"I hope he has moved on," he said. "Did you ever go get that restraining order against him?"

"Unfortunately, I didn't. As I said before, he moved. I don't know where he lives, and you must know where a person lives so they can be served, don't you?"

"It helps, but again, most people can be found. He resides somewhere, for sure."

I wasn't sure if he was hinting at finding out the information for me or not, but I would soon ask him to do it. As I'd said, I just wanted to make sure everything was good with the happy couple, since I hadn't heard a peep out of them since court that day.

"If anything comes up," I said, "I'll let you know. Maybe you can help me put my situation with him to rest, once and for all."

"Hey, anything you need, just let me know."

Damn, I thought as I looked at his lips. He put his cap back on and told me to enjoy the rest of my day. As he walked down the driveway, I called out to him.

"Wait a minute. There is something else." I walked down the driveway to meet him. Behind his glasses, I could see him looking at my nipples that were visible through my top. "I don't know if you do any plumbing work, but one of the sinks inside is clogged. Do you have a minute or two to come inside and take a look?"

A smirk appeared on his face. "It's not my line of work, but let me see how clogged it is. Maybe I can send one of my friends over later to help you out."

"Or maybe, just maybe, you can figure out a way to fix it yourself."

"Maybe so."

I turned, and he followed behind me. As we entered the house, I made my way to the kitchen. I opened the cabinets underneath the sink, inviting him to take a look. He squatted, and I stood right beside him, my pussy was real close.

"Turn on the water," he said. "Let it run for a few minutes."

I did as I was told. The water ran for a few minutes, but the only thing that was clogged was my drain. Officer Wayne knew that too, and when his hands lightly touched my legs, I didn't move.

"Soft," he said, looking up at me. "Just as I had imagined. I don't have time to unclog your drain right now, but I get off around seven or eight. Will you be here?"

"I'll make sure I'm here. And thanks for coming inside to take a look at things for me."

He stood and looked directly at me. "The pleasure was all mine."

I walked him to the door, and after he left, I smiled like a Cheshire cat. I was eager for him to return, and if things went according to my plan, I would soon know where Brent had moved to.

By nine o'clock that night, I had finally gotten my wish. Eric was deep inside of me, stroking me fast with my legs high on his shoulders. He was not a gentle lover. My pussy was taking quite a beating. I wasn't sure if I liked his aggressive approach or not.

"Does it feel good to you?" he asked while pounding my insides.

My head slammed against the headboard, and my legs felt weak as ever. I had no energy as I tried to keep up with his speedy pace. "It's good, but slow down a bit," I managed to say. "Wha . . . What's the rush?"

"I told my wife I would be home by ten. But I wanted to come here and play with you first."

He damn sure wasn't playing. He was doing more than that, and as he started to come, things really got hectic. His head and neck started jerking back and forth. Ass muscles tightened and he flung my legs wide open. While holding them with his hands, he squeezed my ankles and growled like a tiger.

"*Grrrrrrrrl!* Oh, baby, that was good. I knew you would be good. Next time, I want to taste it. I'll let you taste me too."

He would be lucky if there was a next time after that performance. I didn't have one orgasm, not even half of one. While seeing the disappointment on my face, he still got off the bed with pride in his eyes, as if he had done something.

"I'm off work tomorrow, but I already have plans. What if I stop by next week? I'll let you know when, if you want to see me again."

If he could get me the information I wanted, yes, seeing him again would be fine. "You let me know what day and time works for you. Meanwhile, enjoy your day off and don't hurt nobody else with that thing."

When I said hurt, it was all about my feelings. It was a shame that he had a nice-size penis but didn't even know what to do with it. Talk about being disappointed, I unquestionably was. Looking sexy, obviously, didn't mean a darn thing. My encounter with him made me miss Brent even more. And as soon as Officer Wayne left, I returned to my bedroom, played with myself, and then called it a night.

The next day, things took a little turn. I was outside talking to the guy who cut my grass, when all of a sudden, a white woman pulled over to the curb, parking her car. She got out with a tight face. There was no smile, no nothing. I hadn't a clue who she was until she started to spill the beans about why she was there.

"Well, you're just the little homewrecker, aren't you? Eric and I are getting divorced. You can have him, sweetheart, because I'm not the kind of woman who will fight over a man. Not even my husband."

"Neither am I, especially one who doesn't know how to utilize his penis. There is no need for you to divorce him because of me. I don't want him. He's all yours."

"If you didn't want him, you never would've had sex with him. Apparently, you have feelings for him."

"Listen, I had an itch that needed to be scratched. He *barely* scratched it, so I had to take care of the problem myself. Now leave, please. Go home and tell your husband that you forgive him. You're going to do that anyway, so stop wasting your time and mine."

The woman caught me off guard when she shoved me. She knew I was coming after her. That's why she took off down the driveway and hurried into her car. I was so damn frustrated. These women were acting nuts over men—it all made me think about what I had done to Brent. In my defense, again, he deserved it.

Later that day, I was in my spare room sending out some more résumés. I hadn't heard from anyone. I thought that was kind of odd. Clinton said it was hard finding a job in St. Louis, but I didn't think it would be this hard. I had no plans to work at a fast-food joint, or any place like that, but if push came to shove, I had to do whatever I had to do for money. It was getting low. Some of my bills were starting to fall behind.

I had just turned off the computer when I heard a knock at the door. I tightened my robe and went to it. Eric was on my porch with his head hanging low. The last thing I wanted to do was help to soothe the heart of a cheater, but what the hell? I wanted some company, so I opened the door.

He leaned against the doorway with his hand in his pocket. "I apologize for my wife coming over here. I had no idea that she had been keeping her eyes on me. She was out of line, and I hope her visit didn't upset you. More than anything, I hope it didn't interfere with us."

"Actually, it didn't. And, sometimes, I get that a woman needs to get certain things off her chest. I guess she did, so now what, Eric? Are the two of you going to work it out, or is that divorce really going to happen?"

He walked inside and closed the door behind him before answering my question. "Don't know, and I really don't care. We've had problems for years."

That's what they all said. I didn't have time to listen to this mess, but I had to play nice. I walked into the sitting area, turned on the TV, and then plopped on the couch. Eric sat next to me, throwing his leg over mine.

"Do you mind if I stay the night with you?" he said, then sighed. "We've been arguing all day. I just don't want to go home and face my headache."

"You're more than welcome to stay here, but be sure to leave your gun on the table. If your wife keeps showing up and causing problems for me, I'll be forced to use it. So think about that, before you decide to get some rest."

He laughed; I didn't. If he wanted to take the risk, oh well.

"You wouldn't hurt nobody," he said. "You're too sweet. I noticed that about you the first time I saw you. And after that sex we had last night, I can understand why Mr. Carson is having a difficult time letting go. Have you heard anything from him?"

"As a matter of fact, he called me earlier today. He said if I didn't meet up with him this weekend, there would be a price to pay. I think I'd better go get that restraining order against him on Monday. And if you can, see what you can do about finding an address for him. That would help me out a lot. He can be served the restraining order and that should be enough to put fear in him so he'll leave me alone."

"That or possibly a bullet in his head. Niggas like him don't know when to quit sometimes.

And they only learn a lesson when they're six feet under. I've seen cases like this time and time again. A nigga who puts his hands on a woman doesn't deserve to live. And every time I'm called to a domestic violence scene, I make sure those fools get what they deserve. Brent better not ever show up while I'm here. If he does, that'll be a bad move on his part."

Eric was talking like one of those dirty cops. But there was no question that he was what I needed to shut down Brent for good. Then again, that all depended on how well things were going with him and Lajuanna. Hopefully soon, I'd be able to find out.

Eric and I sat quietly, watching a suspense/mystery thriller. It was really good, and after it was over, I got up to pour us some wine. He removed the wineglasses from my hands and set them on the table. Then he moved me over to the couch and kneeled between my legs. With his hand touching the belt on my robe, he looked at me.

"Someone real close to me told me that you said my dick wasn't all that. That's what I heard through the grapevine, and she also said you had a severe itch that needed to be scratched. Since you think I didn't utilize my penis well, maybe my mouth can do a little better and make you change your mind about me."

My robe fell open, exposing my nakedness. Eric scooted down lower, and as he spread my legs wide, his tongue slithered inside of me. I gasped and sucked in my shaky stomach.

"I only told her that so I wouldn't hurt her feelings. You know how it is when you just want somebody to go away. You'll say anything."

Eric didn't respond. He turned his tongue in my pussy, causing me to see the light. I had a much-better opinion of his performance, and if he didn't know how to utilize his penis, he surely knew how to work his tongue. He pressed my legs against my stomach while feasting on me as if I was a full-course meal. I could barely control myself. My body started to shake, I squeezed my teary eyes together.

"Call your wife and allow me to correct myself," I shouted. "This is guuuud, baby. Damn good and . . . and you can stay the night with meeee any time!"

All Eric did was laugh.

Chapter Thirteen

Eric and I had been kicking it for the next several days. He surprised the hell out of me when he stopped by in his police car to give me the information I needed. I leaned against his car, smoking a cigarette because my nerves had gotten pretty bad. This job situation was eating away at me, as was the fact that I hadn't heard one word from Kendal. Not one damn word.

"I think this is it," Eric said, giving me a piece of paper. "Has he contacted you again?"

"I don't know why you continue to ask me that, but, yes, he has called. While I was at the grocery store yesterday, I swore I saw him, from a distance, sitting in his car. I walked toward the car, and that's when it sped away."

"Well, go get that restraining order today. And do not go to his house unless I'm with you. Understood?"

"Sure."

"I mean it, Abby. You have no reason to go there, but just in case, at least take me with you so I can really scare him."

"I think that may be a good idea. I'll go get the restraining order, and you can take him a copy of it too."

"No problem. Now, go handle your business. We'll go there later. And then, we'll continue what we started the other night. I'm glad you've gotten accustomed to my handcuffs."

I flicked the cigarette butt in my grass. "And I'm glad you've learned how to fully satisfy my needs."

We both laughed, and before he drove off, I bent over to give him a kiss. I looked at the address written on the piece of paper. I had no idea where it was, so I went inside, Googled it, and the information came up. The area he now lived in wasn't bad. It was a downgrade from the Clayton area, and was much closer to me than I would have thought. With it being less than twenty minutes away, I hurried to change clothes so I could do a quick drive-by. After that, I was going to go get a restraining order against him. He hadn't bothered me one bit, but what the hell? With all of the things I'd had against him, I would be issued one in a heartbeat.

Twenty minutes later, I slowly drove by the two-story brick home that was surrounded by many trees. It sat far back from the curb, and there were several steps to climb before reaching the front door. A swing was on the porch, and when I saw Lajuanna's car parked in the driveway, I knew I had the right house. I wanted to drive by a few more times, just to see if she would come outside. I figured Brent wasn't there, and if he had gotten another job, I wondered where it was. That information would come soon enough. In the meantime, I did what Eric advised me to do and drove to Clayton to get my restraining order. The process was long, but at the end of the day, it was issued. I had to call Eric, just to let him know that it had been done.

"I got it," I said with excitement in my voice.

"Got what?" he spoke in a whisper.

"The restraining order. Were you busy?"

"Yeah, I'm in the middle of writing this stupid, fool-ass nigga a ticket. Let me finish this and I'll call you back. Better yet, I'll see you a little later. Then, we can go handle that."

"Okay. But be nice and don't hurt nobody, okay?"

"I'll try, but you already know how these fools are."

Eric was a mess. I didn't like how he spoke about black folks, black men in particular. He always seemed to degrade them, but when it came to Brent, I really didn't care. Maybe he just didn't like men who abused women. He'd already made that clear.

Eric showed up around seven that evening. I was already dressed to go, and for the first time, we rode in his police car together. He seemed real cocky, and as some people waved and spoke, he didn't bother to reply. He did, however, turn his head when he saw a young black chick carrying some groceries, and when he saw another one standing outside of a convenience store. I didn't say one thing to him, because after our business was done, I intended to get rid of him.

"Which house is it?" he asked while driving slowly down the street.

"Go a few more houses down. I think it's the one on the left. But let me look at the address to be sure."

Eric pulled in front of the house I pointed to, and then he did a U-turn in the middle of the street, just so he could park on the other side. He held a copy of the restraining order in his hand and looked at me.

"Don't touch anything in here and please don't get out of the car. Crouch down and don't let him see you. I'll leave the windows down just so it won't get so stuffy."

"Thanks," I said. "Good luck."

"He's the one who's going to need it."

Eric got out of the car, cocky as ever. I watched his bowlegged self jog across the street and hike the numerous steps to the front door. Brent's car was now in the driveway. I assumed he was home. Minutes later, someone came to the door. I didn't know who it was until I saw Brent standing on the porch with Eric. My heart melted—I was still so in love with Brent. I wanted to rush out of the car, beg for his forgiveness, and ask him if we could just start all over again. After all that had happened, I knew his answer to that would be a big fat no.

Eric talked to Brent while tapping the piece of paper against his hand. I leaned in closer, just to see if I could hear. I didn't hear much, until Brent's voice got loud.

"I can't believe this shit! My wife and I have been doing our own thing. We haven't bothered anybody! When is this shit going to stop? Please tell me when it will end? How is she allowed to get away with this, and why does everyone believe her?"

Just then, Lajuanna came outside. Her voice was softer, so I couldn't hear what she was saying to Eric. All he did was listen, but soon, Brent started yelling again.

"Bullshit! I'm not taking anything. To hell with her, you, and that damn restraining order!"

He snatched the restraining order from Eric's hand, ripping the paper into shreds. Eric grabbed him by the collar, and that was when Lajuanna tried to step between them.

"Stop it!" she yelled. "We get the picture, and he'll stay away from her, for sure!"

"You're damn right he will," Eric said while still holding Brent's shirt. "Leave her alone and don't ever call her again. I'm going to keep my eyes on you, nigga. If I see you following her, you *will* be arrested. This time, you'll be spending more than just five lousy days in jail!" He shoved Brent backward and left the porch.

I was so pleased how Eric conducted himself. He had earned a big reward coming tonight. Brent and Lajuanna went back inside. I heard the door slam, and when Eric got in the car, he quickly sped off.

"Ole punk-ass fool. He tried to get tough, but a man who puts his hands on a woman ain't shit."

"No, he's not. I noticed that that tends to upset you a lot. Do you have any history behind all that aggression?"

"Absolutely, yes, I do. My father used to beat my mother. He'd have her face black and blue sometimes. I watched that shit play out for many years. Then, one day, my mother got tired, and she just upped and shot him. He didn't die, but he damn sure got the message. Let's hope that Brent just got the message too."

"I hope so. I really and truly hope so."

Finally, I got a call from a job that I had just applied for a few days before. It was right after Eric told me where Brent was now working, at a rental car company as an assistant manager. I wanted that position, but instead, I applied for a customer service position where the pay wasn't so bad. It was in another department; therefore, I assumed that Brent wouldn't be the one interviewing me. I'd gotten a call from a white guy named Chris. He sounded very nice over the phone, and when I arrived for my interview, he was even nicer.

"Come this way," he said, walking down a long hallway. "Follow me."

I followed Chris into his office. He closed the door and invited me to have a seat in front of his desk. The interview got underway, where he mentioned the required job responsibili-

ties, as well as the pay. He inquired about my
background experience, and when I told him
I'd worked in management for several years, he
appeared interested. The only thing that was a
setback was when he said he'd check my references. In an effort not to mention Mrs. Thiele,
I had typed a false name and number on my
application. I hoped and prayed that he wasn't
thorough with checking references.

Other than that, I had sold him. I made him
laugh, made him look lustful, and there was no
question that he was impressed. So impressed
that he offered me the job right on the spot.

"Another management job may open up in
another month or two. And if everything goes
well, you should apply for that, just to earn more
money."

"If you don't mind me asking, what is the
starting pay for assistant managers?"

I was just trying to find out Brent's salary, in
addition to knowing how beneficial the position
could be for me.

"It's usually based on experience, but most
of our assistant managers start at fifty or sixty
thousand a year."

I hated to hear that. No wonder he and his
wife had moved. Things had been looking up.
The pay he'd made as a teacher couldn't touch
that.

"That sounds great," I said. "I do want to apply for a management position, but in the meantime, I plan to work my position like you've never seen it done before. Thank you so much for the opportunity, Chris. You don't mind if I call you Chris, do you?"

He blushed while holding his hands behind his head and gazing at my legs that were crossed. "Not at all. As long as I can call you Abby."

I held out my hand. "Deal."

We both laughed. Chris stood and asked if I wanted anything to drink. "How about a soda, water, something? I need you to complete some paperwork, and then you're free to go. But before you leave, I want to introduce you to our team. We have three teams here. Even though we all work separately, we're really all in this together."

"Sounds good to me. And I'll have a Diet Coke, Chris. Thank you."

He left the office, returning ten minutes later with the Diet Coke and papers for me to fill out. I sat at a table in his office, completing the paperwork and taking sips from the soda. Every now and then, I looked up and saw Chris staring at me. He'd smile, and I'd smile back. Deep inside, he made me cringe. I was sick of men like him, who only wanted one damn thing.

"I think I'm all done," I said, standing up. "Please look it over to see if I missed anything."

He looked over the paperwork and nodded. Afterward, we confirmed my start date, which was tomorrow. We then left his office, just so he could introduce me to the team. I met several white women, two were black. An Asian woman worked the front desk, and the rest of the offices were filled with white men. That was . . . until we got to Brent's office. Chris knocked on the door, and a few seconds later, Brent said, "Enter."

Chris walked in; I came in behind him. Brent was on the phone, but when he saw me, his whole body locked in place. He looked at me as if he had seen a ghost. His conversation came to a halt. Mouth didn't move, nothing. He didn't even blink.

"Were you busy?" Chris whispered. "We can always come back. I just wanted to introduce you to our new employee, Abby."

Brent finally blinked and stood up. "I—I'll take care of that for you tomorrow," he said to the caller. "Just give me a little time to look into it."

After that, Brent dropped the phone on the receiver. He cleared his throat and kept staring at me. "Uh, Abby, nice to meet you. When do you start?"

"Tomorrow," I said with a smile. "First thing tomorrow morning."

Brent stepped around his desk and folded his arms as he sat against his desk. He looked so delicious to me. It looked as if he had been doing a little more working out.

"So, you'll be in Chris's department, right?"

"Yes. I'm looking forward to working for him. He really seems like a nice guy."

Chris blushed again, bragging. "Yes, she'll be working for me. I'm going to walk her outside, but before you leave today, you and I need to meet about something important. Will you have time for a brief meeting?"

"I should, maybe after lunch. I was on my way out in about five or ten minutes."

Brent looked at me and winked. I guess that was a hint for me to hang around. I extended my hand to his, but all he touched was the very tip of my fingers. Bastard.

"Nice meeting you," I said. "Take care."

"You too."

I gave it all I had when I strutted out of his office, swaying my curves from side to side. Chris walked me to the door, and after another thank you and see you tomorrow, I left. I sat in my car, waiting for Brent to come outside. And just in case he got aggressive with me, I checked my glove compartment to make sure the pocketknife I had taken from his house was still in there.

It was.

Several minutes later, Brent walked out the front door. He searched the crowded parking lot, and when I blew my horn, he headed my way. I unlocked the door for him. He got inside, slamming the door real hard, before he tore into me.

"Just when I think you've moved on, here you come again. Just tell me whatever I need to do to get you out of my hair. Whatever it is, I will do it. How much, Abby, can I pay you to stop this?"

"Really? You want to pay me? I don't think you mean that."

"I do. I swear I do. Whatever you want . . . anything."

"I don't want your money. Besides, you could never pay me enough to cure the hurt you caused me. And if you're willing to do anything for me, you already know what that is. Leave your wife and come back to me."

"Anything but that."

"That's all I want. I want us as a couple again. If that means we have to creep behind her back, so be it. I'm willing to do that too."

Brent sat silently for a minute. "You know what I don't understand, Abby?"

"What's that?"

"You're such a beautiful woman. You could have nearly any man that you want. Poor Chris in there so excited about you that his dick was about to bust in his pants. But, why me? Why do you keep fucking with me? Why can't you just let me go?"

"I have let you go, but you're the one who keeps messing with me."

"Messing with you how?"

"You keep calling me and hanging up. You keep following me around. I can feel your presence, and I have seen your car a few times too."

"That's not true. It's only in your imagination. After your performance in court, I haven't called you, not once. And I've never followed you."

I shrugged my shoulder. "Well, maybe it's your wife calling me. Maybe it's her driving your car. I don't know, but something is going on. That's why I got the restraining order. I seriously thought it was you. I want to move on too, and for the record, it is totally a coincidence that I interviewed here today. I had no idea that you worked here."

Brent pursed his lips. I guess he didn't believe me. "I don't believe that for one minute. Nor do I believe my wife is calling you or following you."

"Why wouldn't you believe it? You're the one who said she was capable of killing me. And with her background in the service, I'm sure she knows how to utilize some major weapons. I just couldn't take a chance, and I had to do whatever to protect myself."

"How are you protecting yourself right now? With a restraining order being issued, I'm not supposed to be this close to you. Therefore, you can't accept your new position. Don't show up tomorrow, and when Chris calls, tell him you found another job."

I rolled my eyes at Brent. "Please. I'm not doing that. It took me too long to find a job. You'll just have to stay as far as you can away from me, and what we'll do is just stay out of each other's way. That'll work for me, if it works for you."

"Nothing works for me. If I go in there right now and tell Chris all that has happened between us, I'll be the one fired. If I go to the police, they won't do shit. You really destroyed my house with that water, and in the end, I got blamed for it. I had to pay out of my ass, and the landlord wasn't happy."

I pretended that I didn't know what he was talking about. "What water? I don't know anything about water."

Brent just shook his head. "I'm not going into details, because you already know exactly what I'm talking about. I don't know how to get through to you, Abby, and if I could take back some things, I damn well would."

"Well, you can't, but look at the bright side. You and I are in this car talking, and we're not even yelling at each other. That's progress, I don't care what you say. So think about what I said. Me and you again—someway or somehow, make it possible. Now, I have to go. I have a date with a man I consider the devil."

Brent sighed, then opened the car door. I felt good about our conversation. Maybe, just maybe, things were starting to look up again. In the meantime, it was time for Eric to go fly a kite. Almost like clockwork, Eric was at my door. He came inside, dressed in his uniform and holding a walkie-talkie near his mouth.

"Let me repeat the number again, Frances. Then you can pass it along."

"Go ahead," she said. "I'm listening."

He repeated a number that she, in return, confirmed. After that, he attached the walkie-talkie to his holster and leaned in for a kiss.

"I've been waiting to touch those sexy lips all day," he said. "They're always sweet and juicy, as are other things relating to you."

I fake smiled, knowing that it was fun while it lasted, but it was time to call it quits. I wouldn't end it the way Brent had ended it with me. And there was certainly a better way to put closure to a relationship. I took Eric by the hand, escorting him to the sitting room.

"Listen, babe, we need to talk. I've had some things on my mind lately, and I think it's time for me to get them off my chest."

Eric sat back on the couch and started to undo his shirt. A wife beater was underneath it, so he kept that on.

"What's on your mind?" He pulled me close to him and rested his arm around my neck. His foot was pressed against the edge of my table, and he still had on his polished leather work shoes.

I rubbed his hand that was already cuffed over my breast. "I promised myself that I would never get involved with a man who was married. And no matter how hard I try, I can't forget the look on your wife's face when she came here. She was severely wounded. Hurt was all in her eyes, and it doesn't make me feel good that I'm the one contributing to her pain. I recently got involved with another man who was married. His wife got upset, and she killed the two of them. They—"

Eric quickly cut me off. "What was his name?"

"Clinton. Clinton Jackson. Do you know him? He lived on the Southside."

"Yep, I know him. I had many encounters with him, only because he was involved with a chick who lived in my jurisdiction. She was always calling the police on him. And that crazy chick." He paused as if he was in thought. "Damn, I can't remember her name."

"Velma?"

"Yes, that's it. She was always coming to that woman's house to start fights. When I heard about her killing him, it was no surprise to me. That nigga had it coming. He was around here fucking a lot of women, and word on the street was he was HIV. You didn't have sex with him, did you?"

I hurried to clear things up. "No, we never had sex, but we were friends. I had a few encounters with Velma too. She never told me she was his wife though. Neither did he."

"The news got it wrong. They're always getting things wrong. They weren't married at all."

"They may not have been married, but you are. I know that you and your wife are still together, so don't lie. I've just come to the conclusion that I don't want to do this anymore, unless you can show me that the two of you are divorced. Your word isn't good enough. I need to see papers; papers with a seal or a filed date stamped on it."

He removed his arm from around me, and then sat up. As he rubbed his hands together, he was in thought. "My wife and I are still together. But she's been complaining for years about this and that. She's not going anywhere, and that's the truth. As for me and you, just hang in there. Don't make this thing between us so serious."

I hated to lie, but I didn't need anyone in the way when Brent and I got back together. "It is serious, Eric. My feelings are involved, and I feel as if I'm falling in love with you. If she's not going anywhere, it doesn't mean that I'm not. So, please, allow me to walk without any hassles or regrets. We had fun, didn't we? But there are times when the path ahead doesn't look so clear."

"At the end of the day, you're right," Eric said, then he stood up. "I've never forced a woman to do anything that she didn't want to do. And if you feel as if we need to move on, what else can I say?"

"Not much, I guess."

This seemed too easy. I thought Eric was going to turn around and punch me in my face. Instead, he grabbed his shirt and put it on. As he buttoned it, he stared at me.

"You must be back with your ex or you've found yourself another man. I don't believe for one minute that this is about my wife. You've never been concerned with her. Now, all of a sudden, she's a big deal. But the one thing that I don't do is argue and fight with women. Men, that's a different story. There are too many of you out there, and quite frankly, baby, I have a lot to choose from."

I didn't bother to comment. As long as he was leaving, that was good enough for me. I didn't even waste my time walking him to the door. But after he left, I locked it and returned to my bedroom. I lay across the bed, sighing from relief. Brent was on my mind. I wondered how well he and I would get along at work. Tomorrow couldn't get here fast enough.

Chapter Fourteen

The answer to my question was confirmed a few days later. Brent and I got along well. For the most part, he stayed out of my way, and I stayed out of his. We spoke to each other here and there, but when I asked if he'd made a decision about spending time with me, he replied, "Not yet, but soon."

His comment gave me hope. The way we got along gave me hope as well. I was starting to feel at peace, even though that daughter of mine was no longer in the picture. I thought about Kendal a lot. Even considered going back to Barbara's house to speak to her. But deep down, I knew it would be a waste of time. And if Kendal wanted to talk, she knew where to find me. I was still at the same address and was back on track with my bills.

The only little downside at work was Chris. He flirted with me a lot, and even though I was just okay with it, some of the things he'd said rubbed me the wrong way. Filing a harassment suit was in the back of my mind, and if things got too out of hand, I would do what I had to do. The only reason I hadn't done anything yet was because I loved being this close to Brent. I didn't want anything to jeopardize our chances of possibly getting back together. He seemed as if he may have wanted that too, and for him to be so in love with his wife, not once did I see her here. No one even knew who she was, and when I inquired about him to some of my coworkers, they said they didn't even know he was married. They admitted to seeing his ring, but for his wife to not even show up here was kind of odd. Maybe he would bring her to the Christmas party tomorrow. Then again, maybe he didn't want her to know that I was working with him. That made more sense. He didn't tell her because he knew, behind closed doors, I would be his little secret.

I said good-bye to everyone for the day, and as I was walking to my car, Brent called after me. I turned around, smiling as he headed my way.

"Hey, you got a minute?" he said.

"For you, I always do."

This time, we got into his car, instead of mine.

"Are you going to the Christmas party tomorrow?"

"I was planning on it. Are you?"

"Yeah, I'll be there. I may be late, but I'll be there."

"Why are you going to be late?"

"Because I promised Lajuanna that I would go somewhere with her first. We've been arguing a lot lately, and nothing I do seems to do make her happy these days."

"I can't say that I'm sorry to hear that, because I'm not. I wish you would go ahead and end it with her. You never told me why the two of you separated to begin with. Maybe it was a bad idea for the two of you to get back together again."

Brent looked straight-ahead while tapping his finger on the steering wheel. "The reason why we were separated was because she cheated on me with her sergeant while in the service. She got pregnant by him too. When she lost the baby, everything went downhill. He wasn't there for her, and she came running back to me. I didn't want to take her back, but I was so in love with her. Every time I left to go out of town, I went to her place so we could try to work things out. Slowly but surely, we were able to piece our marriage back together. That's why I wound up breaking your heart. I'm really sorry, Abby. Now that things aren't going as she and I had hoped, I'm starting to feel as if I made some serious mistakes."

I wanted to jump for joy, but Brent seemed so hurt that I didn't want to rub him the wrong way. "You did make a huge mistake. A lot of mistakes, Brent, and had I known all of this, maybe things could have been different. But, just so you know, I'm still here for you. And whenever you're ready for me, just let me know."

"I appreciate that. I'll see you at the Christmas party. From what I hear, the parties are a lot of fun. Just do yourself a favor and stay away from Chris. That man is in love with you. There are times when I just want to tell him that you . . ." he paused.

"That I'm what?"

"That you're already taken."

If he never got my hopes up before, he just did. I wanted to reach over, hug Brent, and give him the biggest kiss ever. But in due time that would happen. First things first. And to speed things along, maybe I needed to think of a plan to help him get rid of his wife for good.

The Christmas party lived up to the hype. It was a blast. It was at the Hilton, where many of my coworkers were so toasted that they had to stay the night. I was tipsy, but I was able to handle my liquor. Brent had been drinking a lot too, but Chris had gone overboard. As I was coming out of the ladies' room in my red silk dress, there he was standing by the water fountain. His brown hair was sweaty, tie was undone, and shirt was wrinkled. He'd been dancing all night, clowning and acting a fool. His date seemed a little embarrassed, but when she started drinking, they fit each other very well. I was shocked to see that she was a black woman. Seemed as if Chris had a thing for women like me.

"Hiii, Beautiful," he slurred as I attempted to walk past him. "Are you having a good time?"

"Fabulous time. I needed this for sure. It's been a long time since I've partied this hard."

"Me too. I was looking for you so we could dance. Do you want to dance later?"

"Maybe, but not right now, Chris. I just want to chill, listen to the good music, and chat with the others."

He took a sip from the bottle of beer in his hand. His eyes stayed locked on me. "Anything else you want to do? I mean, you're so freaking sexy, man. I . . . I think I'm in love. I was hoping that we could kind of hook up, if you know what I mean."

"Of course, I know what you mean. But I'm dating someone right now, Chris. If I wasn't, then we could definitely hook up. But the relationship I'm in is pretty serious. We've been talking marriage, so don't get your hopes up."

Chris shrugged, then he moved closer to me. He lifted the beer bottle, placing it at the top of my chest, then lowering it between my meaty cleavage that was on display. "I can be just as good to you as your man is. And being with me has great rewards. You'll get raises, more money, more vacations, and everything. Just think about it for a while and let me know. Meanwhile, would it be possible for me to have one little kiss? Just one? One for the holiday?"

I backed away from Chris, but he reached out and grabbed my waist. He pulled me close to him, and when he puckered, that's when Brent spoke up.

"Chris, go have a seat. You're drunk, man, and you're starting to make a fool of yourself."

Chris laughed, then he released me. He stumbled backward, took another sip of the beer, and looked at Brent.

"Daaaamn. I almost lost control of myself. But she's so beautiful that I"—he paused to belch—"I almost lost it. It's easy to get lost in a woman like that. Don't you think so, man? She's perfect, isn't she?"

His words were on point, but all Brent did was look at me, then back at Chris. "She's a sweet woman," he said. "Now, go sit down or go get yourself a room. You shouldn't be driving like that, you know."

"No, no, I won't. I already got a room. And, sweetheart," he said, looking at me, "if you want to join me, my room number is 218. My date will be there, but if you show, she's going home."

Chris laughed as he stumbled away.

I was going to be laughing too. As soon as I filed sexual harassment charges against him. I'd just about had enough; a person could only be so nice.

"Sorry about that," Brent said. He had been drinking too, but he handled himself a whole lot better than Chris. "Do you want to go back inside and dance? I know you're not leaving already, are you?"

"Of course not. Like I told Chris, I haven't had this much fun in ages. I plan on getting it in tonight."

Brent laughed. I followed him back into the ballroom where the party was. The music was loud, many people were on their feet dancing, and the floor was pretty crowded. Brent and I squeezed in and started partying away. He laughed, and so did I. We did the bump, the jerk, and the butt, as the DJ kicked up old-school songs.

I couldn't believe we had started to get along again, and more than anything, I was glad he had forgiven me. He hadn't said so yet, but that was pretty obvious. I planned on apologizing to him too. He needed to know why I did what I did. I just didn't want to give up on us, because I knew, deep down, we were meant to be together. Tonight proved just that. Who would have ever thought that after all that had happened, we would be standing here dancing and laughing our asses off?

"Shake it, girl," Brent said as I held my hands in the air, rocking my body to the rhythm.

Chris watched us from afar, but I wasn't even tripping off him tonight. My thoughts were on Brent. I hoped he was staying that night. Then again, he probably had to go home to that monster.

"Phew," I said, wiping sweat from my forehead as we left the dance floor. "That was crazy."

"Yes, it was."

Brent pulled back a chair for me to sit down. He sat next to me. There were two other women at the table, but they were deep in a conversation about their favorite reality TV show.

"So," Brent said, "what are you doing after you leave here?"

"I'm going home. Need to get some rest, and I just may get up and go to church tomorrow. Things are looking up, and I'm not trying to look back."

"Neither am I, but, uh, speaking of going back, I was wondering if you wanted to stay here tonight? I got a room, and I really don't want to be by myself."

I was totally shocked by Brent's offer. Things were moving rather quickly. Even though I wanted to get back with him, I had to find out what was really going on with him and his wife. I wanted him to be done with her for good. That way, she could never come back into our lives and cause him to do what he'd done before.

"I don't mind staying here with you, but what about your wife? Isn't she going to come looking for you?"

"She doesn't know I'm here. Besides, I think she's seeing someone else again. She's too busy with him, she doesn't have much time for us anymore."

He sounded pitiful, but that's what he got for dumping me for her. If he had done the right thing and stayed with me, we could've been on top of the world by now. Deep down, I was pissed by his stupidity, but I was happy that things seemed to be falling apart between the two of them.

"Brent, you need to let her go for good. This is the second time she's cheated on you. How can you stand by and let that happen? If a woman doesn't want you, she just doesn't want you. What can you do? Do you love her that much where you're the one who keeps losing out? I almost don't have any sympathy for you because you never should have taken her back to begin with."

He looked around, then swallowed hard. "I know, but you know what? Let's not talk about Lajuanna for the rest of the night. We've been having a good time, so let's continue. I'm shutting it down in about another hour or so. My room number is 311. Come there whenever you're ready and try not to let Chris see you. He'll be real jealous."

We both laughed. Brent got up and walked away. He continued to mingle with the others, but I sat at the table in deep thought. I didn't trust Brent. I didn't trust that if we got back together, that he would depart from Lajuanna for good. I saw a repeat of what he'd done happening again. And with that in mind, I prepared myself to do whatever to get rid of Lajuanna for good. That way, he'd never be able to go back to her.

Feeling pretty good, I got up and danced again. I drank a little more too, and the food was so delicious that I chomped down on some more of that as well. I saw Brent giving his good-byes, and twenty or so minutes after he left, so did I. I took the elevator to the third floor, and as I walked to his room, there was a smile on my face. I just couldn't imagine this moment ever happening again. Brent and I alone, in the same room, and hopefully, making love to each other once again. I was so ready for this. More so when I knocked on the door and he opened with his shirt off. He opened the door wide, and after I walked into the room, he stood behind me. He secured his arms around my neck, and when his lips touched my neck, I sucked in a deep breath. I loved this man. He was always so gentle. His touch was everything. That's why I just couldn't do without it.

"After all the drinking you've done," he said in a whisper, "you still smell good."

I laughed, but only for a little bit. Things turned more serious when he started to unzip the back of my dress. His hands massaged my mountains, and before I knew it, my dress hit the floor. I turned to face him. My breasts were smashed against his chest as I gazed into his eyes.

"Please don't hurt me again. You know how badly I want this, and after we have sex, I'm going to want this even more."

"I want this too, baby. But let's not focus or talk about the past tonight. Let's just focus on the moment—on what's about to take place right now."

I did just that, and as Brent led me back to the bed, I lay on it. He lay over me, but as he started to kiss my neck, there was rapid knocking at the door.

"Damn," he said. "I hope that's not that stupid fool, Chris. Did he see you come in here?"

I shrugged my shoulders. "I don't think so, but he's been lurking around all night. Go get rid of him, and hurry back to me."

I sat up on the bed in nothing but my panties. Brent didn't bother to look through the peephole or ask who was on the other side. All he did was pull the door open. And when he did, the door hit him right in the face. He staggered away from it, and Lajuanna walked inside. The first thing she did was look at me on the bed. Her eyes fired bullets at me as she stared.

"Well well well," she said. "I see the two lovebirds have managed to hook up once again."

Brent spoke up before I did. "It's not like that," he said. "I, we were just . . . just chilling."

Technically, we weren't, but okay. I kept my mouth shut and didn't say a word. I predicted how this would turn out. Brent was going to give his wife exactly what she wanted.

"Is this what *chilling* looks like? And out of all the women, Brent, you just couldn't leave her alone, could you? After all she did, here you are, back between her legs and saying to hell with me."

I tried to bite my tongue, but couldn't. "What else is he supposed to do, if you're the one out there cheating on him? Enough is enough. A man can only take so much."

She held her chest and laughed. "Is *that* what he told you? That I was the one who had been cheating on him? No no no, sweetheart. There are always two sides to every story. And you should hear the side of a woman before you ever believe the side of a man. Don't you know that by now?"

Brent hurried to speak up. "Listen, why don't you just leave and we'll discuss this when I get home. I'll be there shortly, okay?"

He tried to rush her out, but she had so much more to say. "So, *I'm* the one who needs to leave again? And how many discussions do we need to have about your recklessness? If this was the plan, you could have left me where I was, Brent.

Why didn't you just leave me alone and continue on with your whorish ways?" She turned to look at me. "Just so you know, I've never cheated on my husband. I've been nothing but faithful to him, but every time I look up, there he is with someone else. So, you're not the only one, sweetie, trust me. His list is long, and—"

Brent had heard enough. He cut her off and grabbed her arm. "Out, Lajuanna. Get out and stop all this lying. You know what you did, and you know who you've been with. Stop trying to make this all about me, when you're the one who fucked up."

She laughed and snatched away from him. "You're just as crazy as she is. But just so you know, I'm *never* leaving you. I'm going to make your life a living hell and take every dime that you have. So, have fun screwing her tonight. I'll see you at home, and if you're not there by midnight, there *will* be consequences."

Lajuanna didn't even look my way again. But after she left the room, the whole mood had changed. I never thought that Brent could've been messing around with other women, but the way he dumped me was so cold that anything was possible. I damn sure didn't want to go through all of this, just for him to see other women. And the more I'd thought about it, I remembered what Jeff the masseur said about Brent. Basically, he referred to him as a whore.

"She's out of her mind." He locked the door and turned to me. "And I hope you don't believe that crap she just said. The failure of our marriage is solely because of her."

"I don't know what to believe, Brent, but I can tell you that I'm not feeling this right now. I want you to think carefully about how you move forward, because I cannot and will not share you with other women. I've been through too much with you and Lajuanna. While I was willing to be the other woman on the side with her in the picture, I'm no longer feeling that way. You need to clean up your mess. Do it now, before it's too late."

He walked over to the bed, pulling me up from it. As he wrapped his arms around me, I felt his love.

"I wouldn't be here with you unless I wanted to be. My wife is a liar. She's always been a liar, and she said those things to upset you. She doesn't want us to be together. She doesn't want me to be with anyone other than her. The sooner I get rid of her, the better. I'm working on it, and if you want to wait a little while longer, I understand. Until then, please, please, please, allow me to make love to you tonight. My dick is so anxious to feel you. I need to feel you right now."

I was finally in a position where I had the upper hand. And it felt good telling Brent, "No."

"Please, Abby, don't leave me tonight."

"I said no. If you really want this, you'll go home and deal with your wife. You'll end it for good. Tell her to get out and divorce her as quickly as you can. I'm not going to be your hotel lover. And the only place we're going to make love again is in *your* bed, at *your* house. I mean it, Brent. So do what you have to do, if this is really what you want."

He stood speechless. I was proud of myself for once. I snatched up my dress, put it back on, and headed for the door. Brent sat on the bed looking lost. I blew him a kiss, telling him I'd see him at work on Monday. He didn't respond.

Chapter Fifteen

Things at work had been crazy. Not only had Chris been getting more and more out of control, but Brent and I had been out of control too. We had been sneaking away to kiss and fondle each other. I would go into his office, just to let him get a few feels and tell me how badly he wanted me. The only thing we hadn't done yet was have sex. I was holding off, just to see what he was going to do. It was the only way to keep the ball in my court. If I gave in, I thought Brent would dump me. I started following him around again, just to make sure there were no other women. And from what I knew right now, Lajuanna had lied. Brent hadn't been with anyone else. I even checked his phone. There was nothing.

On the other hand, she had been the one creeping around. I saw her get into a car with another man, just this morning. I had been following them too, but when I called Brent to tell him where they were, he didn't answer his phone. I sent him a text message, telling him to call me soon. And just as Lajuanna and her lover were getting out of his car, Brent called me back.

"Sorry I missed your call," he said. "I was at the grocery store and didn't hear it ringing."

"I just want you to know that your wife just went into an apartment with another man."

Brent was quiet. He didn't say one word.

"Did you hear what I just said?"

"I heard you, but you're not telling me anything I don't already know. Is he light-skinned, tall, drive a Lincoln truck?"

"Yes, that's him."

"I know. I know him well. His name is Travis. She just can't seem to get enough of him."

I was so frustrated while listening to him. "If that's the case, then what's the holdup, Brent? Why are you still dealing with her? This is crazy."

"It is. Very crazy, and I don't need you doing any private investigating for me. I'm working behind the scenes to take care of everything. Things are not going to happen overnight, but they will happen. You have to be patient with me, okay?"

"I have been patient. More patient than you will ever know. I just don't see why you just can't walk away and be done with this."

"Soon, Abby. I will be done with her soon. Now leave before someone sees you. Call me when you get home, and let's have phone sex, since you don't want us to do the real thing."

That made me crack a tiny smile. "Okay. I'm leaving. Keep your phone nearby. I'll be home soon."

I headed home, thinking about how I could speed things along with Brent and his wife. I knew that the one person who could probably help me was Eric. I hadn't spoken to him since he'd left that day. But just for the hell of it, I called his cell phone to see what was up with him.

"You're not going to believe this," he said. "But I was just sitting here in traffic, thinking about you."

"And I was on my way home, thinking about you. I was thinking that maybe I need to see you again. I also need a little favor. I wondered if you could kind of help me out."

"You already know my schedule. I don't get off until nine. Can I stop by then?"

"That'll be fine."

"Okay. But tell me more about this favor."

"I'll tell you all about it when you get here. I think you're going to like it."

Eric laughed. And after we ended our call, I hurried home so I could indulge in some hot and heavy phone sex with Brent.

"It's your voice," he moaned. "I luuuuuv the way you speak. My dick is so hard right now that it's about to explode. I'm saving the explosion for you, though. I want it all inside of you. Leaking, dripping, raining, and oozing all inside of you. Why don't you let me come over?"

As Brent talked, my fingers were in my panties, tickling my pearl. "I want you to come over, but I also want to come now. My pussy is tingling—bad. It's thumping, dripping, tightening, and making a gushy sound, wishing you were in it. I want you all the way in there, Brent, but not until she's gone. Make her go away. She needs to disappear so that we can finally fuck all day and all night. You *do* want to fuck me, don't you?"

"Yes. I'm fucking you now. Fucking you real good, baby, you should see me. Ahhhhhh!"

The phone dropped. I could hear a bunch of rambling going on. I closed my eyes and released my energy as well. Afterward, I fell back on the bed and called out to Brent.

"I need to go take a cold shower," he whispered. "That felt good, but nothing feels better than being inside of you."

He hung up on me. It felt good that I was back in control of things. I loved that Brent was dangling on my stick. And no matter how badly I wanted him, he had to wait. Wait until I put together my own plan to remove the one person standing in our way.

Unfortunately for me, in order for me to get what I wanted, I had to give something. That something was sex with Eric again. I made sure it was extra good for him, and as he lay underneath me, guiding my hips, I rode him tough.

"Umph umph umph," he said while rubbing my wobbling breasts that wouldn't stay still. "Work that shit, girl. I am loving every bit of this and . . . and I'm glad, so glad, you called."

Eric was successfully stirring my juices as well. He had gotten better sexually, but he still was no Brent. I quickly made him release his buildup, and afterward, I fell next to him in bed. He held me in his arms as I rubbed the minimal hairs on his chest.

"You're always so good to me," I said. "And I'm glad I can count on you when I need to get things done."

"You're damn right you can count on me. With a pussy like that, there are not too many things you can't get from me."

That's exactly what I wanted to hear.

"I hope so, Eric, because I need a huge favor from you. You're the only one who can pull it off, and I trust you, more than I trust anyone."

"You keep beating around the bush. Go ahead and tell me about this favor."

"It deals with Brent's wife. That woman is continuously making my life miserable. I don't know what's wrong with her. She's nothing like your wife, and she refuses to leave me alone. Every time I look up, she's following me, calling me . . . wanting to fight me. I was in the grocery store the other day, and she came from out of nowhere, yelling and screaming at me as if I had done something to her. A restraining order isn't going to help her. She needs to be dealt with. Soon."

"Dealt with how?"

"I . . . I'm really not sure. But you deal with reckless people all the time. How do you handle them? How do you get them to stop doing crazy things that disturb you?"

Eric shrugged his shoulder. "I may pistol-whip a nigga or make him sit in jail for a few days. I've also done some dirty shit that I wouldn't dare tell you about."

I playfully shoved his chest. "No, please, go ahead and tell me. I want to know. What have you done?"

"I can't say. It involves some other officers too, so it wouldn't be wise for me to speak on those instances."

"Okay, but, uh, I'm kind of talking about something like that. You know, something that can silence her for good."

"You mean, you want her killed? Is that what you're saying?"

"If that's what it takes, yes, I do. I really don't see this ending any other way. It's either going to be me who dies or her. I've just never killed anybody. I wouldn't know what to do, and as nice as I am, she would probably talk me out of something like that."

Eric laughed and rubbed my arm. "You are too nice and too sweet too. And I damn sure have the experience to take care of that for you. But I don't know about this, Abby. If it were a man, like her husband Brent, I wouldn't have no problem at all doing it. But when it comes to women, I kind of have a soft spot for y'all."

"I know, but trust me when I say she doesn't act like a lady. She's a real bitch. You saw for yourself how she was when you served Brent that restraining order, didn't you?"

"She was all right. But if she's been doing all this shit to you, maybe I can pull her over one day, threaten her, slap her around a little, and scare the pants off her. That may work."

"Possibly. But it sure would make me feel better if I never, ever had to see her face again. Just think about it, okay? Give it a little more thought, and whatever I can do to speed things along, let me know."

I helped Eric make his decision when I lowered myself and sucked his goods into my mouth. He loved every bit of it. I knew that my skillful performance was leading him closer and closer to making the right decision.

Chapter Sixteen

The decision had been made. It was time to rock and roll. Eric came up with a brilliant plan to do away with Lajuanna. It was a plan that Brent didn't even know about. He had been dragging his feet. I needed action. Action that he hadn't taken thus far, yet he claimed something good was in the works. The night before things were supposed to go down, he and I spent a quiet evening together. He was at my house; he hadn't been there in a very long time. We sat at the dinner table, chomping down on the steak and potatoes I had cooked. I also made a cherry cheesecake, only because it was his favorite.

"You're always spoiling me," he said, dabbing his mouth with a napkin. "I'm going to love spending the rest of my life with you, and in due time, that will happen."

He was starting to sound like a broken record. "You're right about that. It will happen, sooner than you think. I've been patient long enough,

Brent. It's time for action. I'm a woman of action, and I think you already know that."

"Yes, I know, but what exactly does that mean?"

I shrugged my shoulders. "You'll see. Soon you will see, and then, I'll be able to give you everything your heart desires, and more."

As those words left my mouth, the doorbell rang. We looked at each other, knowing that a ringing bell wasn't always a good thing.

"Stay right here. I'll get it," I said.

I made my way to the door, and when I looked through the window, I saw Eric's police car in the driveway. I didn't want him to see me with Brent. I also didn't want to turn him away because he was on the verge of doing something so awesome for me. I opened the door, but as he stepped forward to come inside, I blocked him.

"Just to let you know, I do have company. What's on your mind and why are you here?"

"Company?" he asked, as if I wasn't allowed to have visitors. "I just stopped by to see if we could have a little celebration before the big day tomorrow. I guess you're celebrating with someone else. Who, may I ask?"

He didn't have to ask because Brent came into the living room, standing with his hands in his pockets.

"Am I interrupting something?" he asked.

"Could be," Eric replied. "But, uh, I don't quite get this. I served you a restraining order, so technically, you shouldn't even be here. Question is, what's your purpose?"

I didn't want Eric to start any trouble, so I hurried to speak up. "Brent and I are just having a long-needed conversation. I made him dinner, and we're trying to settle a few things from the past. That's it. Nothing more, nothing less."

I looked at Brent and could tell his thoughts were racing a mile a minute. So were Eric's, but he backed up to the door, placing his hand on the knob. "Outside," he said to me. "Come outside. We need to talk."

I didn't want my plans to fall apart, so I looked at Brent, telling him I would be right back.

"Don't go anywhere, okay? Go turn on some music and get yourself another glass of wine. Just give me a minute, okay?"

He walked away without saying a word. I went outside and stood by Eric's car with him.

"I'm sensing something real fishy going on," he said. "I don't like that nigga being here, Abby. I thought it was over with between the two of you."

"Trust me, it is. We just needed to talk, that's all. And when something happens to his wife, the last person I want him to come to is me. I'm trying to be nice to him, because coming off as bitter will do me no good. I'll be the first person he tells the police to look for when she's gone. I don't want that, so I thought it would be a good idea for him and me to clear the air."

"That's all you'd better be doing is clearing the air with him. I'll be driving by a few more times tonight. He'd better not be here too much longer."

This fool was crazy. Who in the hell was he, trying to call the shots? The only reason I was with his program for the night was because of what he would do for me tomorrow. I had to keep him on my good side, at least until then.

"You don't have to watch me all night, but he will be gone soon. I promise, okay?"

To seal the deal, I leaned in to kiss Eric. My kisses always made him smile; his whole demeanor changed.

"Okay, sexy. I'll see you tomorrow. After all is said and done, the two of us are going to go somewhere nice and celebrate. Celebrate big too."

I winked at him. "You can count on that."

He pulled out of my driveway, and I headed inside to explain this situation to Brent. He didn't hear me come in, so I stood behind a wall in the living room, listening to his conversation as he sat on my couch.

"I do love you," he whispered in a whiny voice. "I'm trying, but you gotta try too, baby. You being with him is killing me. All I want is my wife back. The one I married years ago, who loved me more than anything in the world. Why can't I have her back?"

See, this kind of shit angered me. I wanted to fuck Brent up. He was constantly lying, as if he really wanted to get rid of his wife. But he didn't have to worry anymore. I was going to do it for him, and after I dealt with her, I intended to deal with him and his lies too.

I tiptoed back to the front door, slamming it. And when I returned to the kitchen, his phone was now on the table, as if he hadn't used it. A blank expression was on his face.

"So, what's up with you and that cop? He's the one who served me that restraining order. I have a good feeling that he doesn't like me."

"He doesn't like a whole lot of people, so don't take it personal."

"I *am* going to take it personal, because it's obvious that he's involved with you. How long has this been going on?"

"Brent, it really doesn't matter, does it? All you need to know is that when you're done with your wife, I'll be done with him. But it sounds to me, and from what I just heard, you're still in love with her. You still want her back, but you've been telling me it's almost over."

He swallowed and looked down at the floor. When he looked up, his eyes were watery and his voice softened.

"Have you ever just loved somebody to death and you just didn't want to let them go? I'm sure you have, Abby, and it's a badass feeling. You try everything . . . every little thing, to show them how much you love them. Sometimes, you find yourself so out of character that it scares you. But no matter what, you're willing to fight until the end. The fight may not be worth it, but in your view, you have to do something. I'm at that point in my marriage. I'm fighting, but deep down, I know I need to let go. I'm just trying to hang on to every little day, minute, and second that I have left. But the truth is, and when reality sets in, it's over. There's nothing I can say or do, because it's over. That's why I can clearly say to you that one day, we will be together. But in the meantime, you must know that my heart is so broken. I don't know how long it will take for me to heal."

A slow tear rolled down Brent's face. I had never, ever seen him cry. I could finally see the pain he was in, and every single thing he'd said made sense. I knew exactly how he felt. It was hard to let go of someone you loved so very much.

And as for being out of character, I had been that, and then some. I wanted to fight for him until the very end too, but the only difference between him and me was the outcome would be different. He wouldn't get to hang on to Lajuanna forever. I, on the other hand, would bring him back to life and help him heal from all the hurt she had delivered.

"I thank you for pouring your heart out to me, sweetheart. It means a lot. I know you love her . . . You may always love her, but one day, you'll have to open your eyes and see who has really been in your corner. And when you talk about fighting, I've fought hard for us. I just couldn't give up, and one day, you're going to appreciate everything I've done."

I gave Brent a kiss, trying to make him feel better. He perked up a little, and when he said he'd better go, I didn't stop him because I knew Eric had been waiting on him to leave. I did, however, walk him to his car. We kissed one last time before he drove out of my driveway and down the street.

I saw Eric's police car at the end of the street. And after Brent passed by him, Eric drove away too.

***

The following day, I was up early. I was a bit nervous, but I waited for Eric to call and give me some good news or directions. I finally heard from him around noon. He called to say he was on his way to pick me up so we could go "handle" things.

"I'll be waiting for you. Hurry, please."

"I said I'm on my way."

His attitude was fucked up, but I didn't care. I wanted to get this day over with. It had been a long time coming. I couldn't wait to look Lajuanna in the eyes when Eric blew her damn brains out. Brent would be sad for a while, but I would be there to comfort him. I would be everything that he needed me to be, and as for Eric, well, he would be dealt with at a later day. There was no way for me to keep him around. He knew too much, and as controlling as he was, he would demand so much from me that my head would spin. I didn't want to have sex with any man but Brent. It would just be me and him, and no one else.

I was inside when I heard Eric blow his horn. I grabbed my purse and locked the door on my way out. As I walked to his car, he was on his cell phone. He placed his finger over his lips as a sign for me to be quiet. I got in the car, listening to him lie like hell to his wife about where he was. This whole thing was just sickening. I couldn't get rid of him fast enough, and maybe his wife would thank me for the good deed.

"Sorry about that," he said, ending the call. "She's a pain in the ass!"

"Aren't they/we all? My ex-husband felt the same way about me, but he'd better be thankful that he's still alive."

"Why? Had you wanted him dead too?"

"Plenty of times." I removed a cigarette from my purse, thinking about all of the headaches he'd cost me. "I would've shot him myself, but the only thing that saved him was he was Kendal's father."

"I guess he should consider himself lucky to be alive then."

"Very lucky. He just don't know."

Eric laughed. He turned up the volume on the radio, making small talk with me as we drove to Brent's place. He wasn't supposed to be home. He told me several days ago that he was going to Chicago to see one of his friends. I wasn't sure if he'd told the truth, but when I called him earlier, he didn't answer his phone. All I was concerned about was him being away. Eric and I planned this at the right time, and when he parked on the side of the house, we saw that her car was the only one in the driveway. Eric looked over at me and took a deep breath.

"Are you ready?" he asked, touching his gun that was in a holster.

"More than ready."

As planned, we both got out of the car and headed to the door. Eric knocked, or should I say, banged, pretty hard.

"Who is it?" Lajuanna yelled.

"Officer Wayne. I spoke to you and your husband before. I need to speak to the two of you again."

Lajuanna opened the door with a bowl in her hand. It looked like she'd been stirring some kind of cake mix or something. She looked at me, then at Eric, before opening the screen.

"My husband isn't here," she said in a nasty tone. "What's wrong now? Tell me what all this is about."

"May we come inside? I think there are some important things you and Miss Wilson need to discuss. Maybe after the two of you talk, all of these things that have been going on for quite some time now can be put to rest."

Lajuanna moved away from the door, allowing us to come inside. The second I walked in, I could smell Brent's scent. My eyes scanned the lavish-looking living room that would soon be mine to redecorate. I didn't necessarily like the blue and white colors. I would probably change them to gray, white, and yellow. Other than that, the hardwood floors shined, colorful pictures covered the walls, and the light fixtures were on point. This was a step up from the other place for sure. I couldn't wait to call it home.

"Would the two of you like to have a seat?" Lajuanna asked.

She was being extremely polite. Probably because Eric was a police officer and she was showing him respect. She also didn't want to get arrested. I was sure of that.

"No, we'll stand," Eric said.

"Well, let me go put this bowl back in the kitchen. I'll be right back, then we can talk."

She walked away. Eric examined her back side with a smirk on his face. I wanted to slap the shit out of him for being so disrespectful. But he was his wife's headache, not mine.

Lajuanna came back, wiping her hands on a towel. We all stood in the foyer. Eric was the first to speak up again.

"Your husband is in a lot of trouble," he said to her. "He's been seeing this woman off and on, and just last night, he put his hands on her again. He was warned to stay away from her, as were you. But you continue to harass her, and the last thing I wanted to do was come here and arrest you. As Miss Wilson and I talked about this, we figured that it would be in your best interest to speak up and testify against your husband, if need be. He's going to jail this time, and you will go with him, if you do not cooperate with us."

Lajuanna moved her head from side to side. "I don't want to have anything to do with this," she spoke tearfully. "Brent is his own man, and he does his own thing. Abby just won't leave him alone. It's her own fault for not leaving him alone, and if he's going to be arrested, so be it. I'm not testifying or speaking up for anyone."

"That's what I thought you'd say."

Eric caught her off guard when he lifted his hand, backslapping her so hard that she went flying to the other side of the room. She landed on the floor in shock. Her eyes bugged as she sat up, covering her bloody mouth.

"Oh my God," she cried out. "What are you doing?"

Eric was a bit sinister. I had chosen the right man for the job, but as I watched his whole demeanor change, I knew I had to be careful messing with him. The look in his eyes was devilish. He had no mercy for Lajuanna, and as he kicked her in the chest with his foot, she fell backward. He placed his foot on her neck, pressing down hard so she couldn't breathe. All she made was a gurgling sound while her arms and legs flopped around. I watched with glee in my eyes. Seeing her like this took me back to that day in the courthouse when she had beaten my ass. This was payback for that day, and then some.

"What you say, bitch?" Eric said, laughing. "I can't hear you. Your voice isn't clear."

Lajuanna was using all the strength she had to try to remove his foot from her neck. She couldn't, so she lifted her shirt where a knife could be seen, tucked into her pants. As she struggled to get it, Eric yanked it out. He tossed it over to the side, and then released his foot from her neck. She tried to move away, but he squatted behind her, putting her in a choke hold.

"What were you going to do with that knife, huh? Were you going to try to kill me or kill her?"

She gazed at me with watery eyes—madness and anger were trapped inside. "Nah, you can't kill her. She's too valuable to me, but you, on the other hand, are not. Then again . . ." He touched her breast and squeezed it. "Maybe you *are* valuable."

Eric stood, and while holding her arms, he dragged her across the floor. The plan wasn't for him to rape her, but Eric was so dirty that he had probably thought about doing this all along.

"Noooo," Lajuanna cried out while kicking and screaming as he continued to drag her away. "Don't you touch me! I mean it, damn it! Don't you put your grimy hands on meeee!"

Eric looked at me as I remained in the foyer. I didn't want to see him rape her, so I didn't move.

"I'll be right back," he said with a psychotic look in his eyes. "This will only take a minute or two. Then you'll get your wish."

"Hurry," I said, feeling nervous. I started to bite my nails. "Jus . . . Just shoot her and let's go."

Lajuanna continued to scream and holler as Eric called her all kinds of names. I heard slaps, and as her cries got louder, I knew he was raping her.

"Noooooo," she hollered. There were several *booms;* I guess she was kicking the floor, wall, or something.

"Shut the fuck up!"

Her cries became muffled. His moans got louder. I heard nothing else from her, and after another minute or two, the sound of gunfire rang out, causing my whole body to jump. No doubt, this was tough. I now wished that I hadn't come here. I should have allowed Eric to do this himself, but he suggested that I partake in what he referred to as "the festivities."

He came from the back, zipping up his pants and placing his gun back in the holster. "Done," he said. "Now, let's get the fuck out of here."

I was down with that. We rushed out of the house and hopped in the car. Eric was breathing hard; so was I.

"That wasn't so bad, was it?" He spoke with a wicked grin on his face. "Both of them are history, and you can now live free and move on with your life, Miss Lady."

My face twisted. I looked at him like he was crazy. "What do you mean by both of them are history? I only asked—"

"Yeah, I know. You only wanted me to take care of her, but I took care of him too. After he left your house last night, I followed him and handled him as well."

My stomach felt queasy. I wanted to fucking cry. My heart was beating fast. I could barely speak.

"Wha . . . What did you do to him, Eric? Please, God, no, don't tell me you killed him."

A confused look washed across his face. "I thought that was what you wanted. Didn't you want him dead too?"

"No no no!" I pounded my fist against the dash. "No, Eric! It was *not* what I wanted! I wanted you to kill her, not him! What in the hell did you do to him?" Tears rushed to the rims of my eyes.

This couldn't be happening. There was no way in hell Brent was dead.

"Listen, you'd better calm the fuck down. I did this shit for you!" Eric darted his finger at me. "You need to be a little more appreciative of my hard work. I wanted to make this look like a murder-suicide, so I knocked him off and put him in the basement while she wasn't here last night. After I drop you off, I'm coming back to take her body downstairs with his. Whenever they're found, that's what it'll look like."

I could've died, right then and there. No, this fool didn't kill my Brent. No, he fucking didn't! I hopped out of the car and rushed back inside. I had to see this shit for my damn self. Maybe I could save Brent. Maybe it wasn't too late for him. Damn Eric for doing this! I hoped like hell that what he'd said wasn't true.

Unfortunately for me, when I found the basement door and hurried downstairs, I saw Brent. His body was lying on the cold concrete floor. He was flat on his stomach and wasn't breathing at all. In tears, I ran over to him and fell to my knees. I turned him over and tried to pull his heavy, limp body on my lap.

"I'm sorry, baby," I said, rubbing his handsome face. "I'm sorry that he did this to you. I didn't want him to do this. You have to know that I didn't want this for youuuuu!"

Eric rushed down the stairs, but I paid him no mind. All I wanted was Brent. I lowered my head, covered his mouth with mine, and tried to breathe some life into him.

"Come on, baby," I cried. "Wake up! You've got to get up! I need you. Now that she's gone, I need youuuu!"

"For the record, bitch, I'm not gon' anywhere. And the only person who needs to wake up is you."

My head snapped up. Standing right behind Eric was Lajuanna. My face scrunched, and when I looked down at Brent, his eyes popped open.

"You're done," he said. "This is over, and your ass will be going to jail for a very long time."

What in the hell did he just say?

I was shocked beyond words. This couldn't have been happening—had I really been set up like this? Reality kicked in when Brent stood up and Lajuanna rushed into his arms. She cried hard, as he held her in his arms and rubbed her back.

"It's okay, baby," he said softly. "It's over. It's all over with."

"Thank God," she said. "I hope that bitch rots in hell."

I remained on the floor like a mannequin. That was until Eric came over and lifted me off the floor. He reached for his handcuffs, before placing my hands behind my back.

"You have the right to remain silent. Anything you say can and will be used . . ."

My mouth hung open as I listened to him read me my rights. I stood like a zombie. He was real rough with me too, and when I tried to snatch away from him, he yanked my arms, straightening me up real quick.

"Step forward and let's go," he spoke through gritted teeth. "If you try anything stupid, I *will* hurt you, you understand?"

I didn't doubt him. And as I inched forward, eyeing Brent, Eric yanked my arm. He pulled me up the stairs where I was now in the presence of several more officers, including the white chick who had come to my house, claiming to be Eric's wife. The pieces of the puzzle were finally coming together. I was set up . . . big time.

Chapter Seventeen

As I sat in an interrogation room with my hands cuffed behind my back, Eric sat across from me, leaning back in his chair with a grin on his face. He had been talking shit to me for the past ten minutes, but I hadn't said a word.

"So you see, Abby, the first time I set my eyes on you, I knew you were a liar. Trouble was written all over you. I'm paid to know when people are bullshitting me, and I could see right through you. Not once did you have me fooled, and in addition to that, I'd known Brent from college. He just wasn't the kind of man you were making him out to be. So me, him, and his beautiful wife had a serious discussion one day. They didn't know how to stop you, but I did. You were good, baby. In every single way, you were masterful."

I swallowed the lump in my throat and turned my head to the side. Maybe I had been masterful, but in the end, it surely didn't feel that way. I hated that it had come to this. The last thing I wanted to do was sit there and listen to Eric tell me how I'd been played. He gloated about his little plan, and he just couldn't shut his big freaking mouth.

"I have to ask if all of this was worth it. Was Brent Carson really worth it? You just couldn't leave him alone, even when he told you that he didn't want to be with you anymore. Sometimes, Abby, you just have to walk away. There is a reason for everything, even if it sometimes hurts too damn bad."

I remained quiet, but if he kept at it, I had something for him.

"I'm not saying that Brent's actions were right. He was dead wrong. Wrong for how he treated you, but you shouldn't have done the shit you did. That was totally uncalled for, and somebody could have gotten killed. You were lucky, damn lucky, that it wasn't you. And in the end, you lost out big time. I doubt that you'll ever see your daughter again, and what about your little precious grandbaby? You'll be lucky to see pictures of him. She had a boy, by the way, and you were too busy in Brent's business that you didn't even know that. So, I have to ask you again . . . Was Brent Carson really worth it?"

I answered when I gathered spit in my mouth and shot it at his face. It dripped down his face like a slow tear. He wiped it, then got up and grabbed the back of my neck. He slammed my head on the table, holding me down so I wouldn't move.

"Was he fucking worth it, you stupid bitch? You fucked your life up for what? Nothing! For a man who didn't give a damn about you! He didn't give a shit, Abby, and all you had to do was walk away! You should have left him alone and let him be with the woman he truly loved!"

My face hurt as it was pressed hard against the table. I knew what he said was right, but it was just the way he'd said it that hurt. He released my neck, and when I sat up straight in the chair, tears rolled down my face.

"Aw, so now you want to cry about it. Why are you crying, Abby? It's too late for those tears, and you know it."

The door opened and the white officer, his so-called wife, came into the room. She gave Eric a folder, then she looked at me.

"Is he being nice to you?" she said, waiting for a response. Just to fuck with Eric, I responded to her question.

"No, he's not being nice. But he was real nice when he had his dick in me."

"Well, that's how some men are, sweetheart. They're mean and ugly, like I was when I came to your house that day. And for the record, I would never be married to an asshole like him."

She laughed. So did he.

"Get out of here," he said. "And I have been nice. Real nice, considering all that she's done."

The woman officer closed the door. Eric sat back down to examine what was in the file. He rubbed his chin and nodded his head.

"This doesn't look good, baby. You're in a whole lot of trouble. I have to ask if you even want to call an attorney."

I just stared at him. He knew I was fucked. An attorney couldn't save me; I wasn't about to waste my time or money on one. If the court wanted to assign me a public defender, so be it.

Eric closed the file. "So you still won't talk to me, huh? What if I put you on this table, open those pretty legs, and stick my tongue where the sun don't shine? Will you talk to me then? I would hope so, especially since you always used to talk when we, you know, did the wild thing."

I wanted so badly to tell this fool how bad his sex really was. But what good would that do me right now? None. I kept quiet, hoping that this would all be over with soon. Unfortunately for me, though, Eric tortured the shit out of me. He kept going on and on about what I had done, about Brent, about his wife, about Kendal and my new grandbaby. When Eric spoke of him, it brought more tears to my eyes. I was hurt. Devastated, more like it, because this was all on me. Kendal needed me. I failed her. I failed myself, and I failed her child.

"For the last time," Eric said. "Was your fight to conquer Brent Carson worth it?"

I took a deep breath, looked him straight in the eyes, and finally answered his question.

"With all my heart, yes, he was."

Eric reached out and slapped the shit out of me. My head jerked to the side and hung low.

Not saying another word, he opened the door and walked out.

Chapter Eighteen

Being in orange had become my new black, and being in jail was no picnic. I wanted a do over, but unfortunately for me, I wasn't going to get it. This was now my reality, and now, Brent and his wife had gotten their happily-ever-after. Me, on the other hand, I got nothing. Nothing but a hard-ass bed, terrible food, and mediocre pussy sucking every now and then. The only good days came when Kendal and my grandbaby visited me. They'd only done so twice. She didn't have to, because Lord knows I had dropped the ball on her as a mother. I didn't see it then, but I sure as hell saw it now. I had time to reflect on many things. If I could turn back the hands of time, I most certainly would.

I sat in my orange jumpsuit in the visiting quarters waiting for Kendal and my grandson, Miguel, to come see me. He was adorable, and it always brightened my day just to be able to hold him in my arms. I was sure that Kendal would, eventually, stop bringing him here to see me. But for now, I savored every little minute we had together.

Kendal, on the other hand, was doing well, considering all that had happened. She had a job, she and her boyfriend lived together, and she even mentioned something about marrying him. I would miss that day too, because for the next thirty-five years, this place was my new home.

Feeling kind of bad today, I cracked a tiny smile as Kendal came into the room carrying Miguel on her hip. He was playing with a toy and was already getting so big. I was hurting inside, but just so Kendal wouldn't notice, I did my best to hide my pain very well.

"Hello, Mama," she said as I stood to greet her. "How are you today?"

"I'm hanging in there." I reached out for my grandson, giving him a big kiss. "Muuuuah! Those cute little chubby cheeks are to die for. I love, love, love you!"

Miguel giggled as I sat him on my lap. I looked at Kendal. "I love you too, you know?"

"I do know that, and I wouldn't be here if I thought otherwise. You just made some really bad mistakes, Mama. Real bad, and nothing that anyone said or did could stop you from wanting Brent so badly."

"I know, but can we please not talk about him? I don't want to talk about him right now. I'd rather talk about what you've been up to, how you've been, and what your plans are."

"I'm doing well. I wish I had a better job, but you already know how that is. I'm going to start looking for another one soon, but my search is going to be outside of St. Louis. That's what I came here to tell you. I'm planning on moving away from here because the job market is slow. I can do better in a place like Atlanta, or possibly North Carolina somewhere."

That wasn't good news to me. Kendal was all I had. If she went away, I was sure her visits would come to a halt . . . as would the money she'd been putting on my books.

"It's funny how I'm in a position where I have to count on you to take care of me. And even though your move disappoints me, please go live your life to the fullest. I'll be okay in here. Jus . . . Just visit when you can and be sure to send me some pictures of my grandbaby. I want to see him grow up. Grow into a fine young man." I paused to look at Miguel who was busy with his toy. "Has your father seen him?"

Kendal shrugged. "Only one time, believe it or not. You know how he is. He doesn't have time for anyone but himself. But that doesn't bother me anymore. It is what it is."

I reached over and touched Kendal's hand. "I'm so sorry, sweetheart. We both failed you, but I'm glad that you turned out to be an awesome and caring young lady. If that's because of Barbara, then I have to thank her for that. She came through for me when I didn't have my head on straight."

Kendal tried to spare my feelings. "Listen, Mama, I can't sit here and give Barbara all of the credit. You were a great mother until Brent came along. Something about you changed, and while you don't want to talk about him, we have to. I don't want to push this under the rug any longer, and even though I made many attempts to get through to you before, you just never listened."

"Kendal, if I don't want to talk about him, I just don't want to talk about him. It's best that my memories of him stay buried. I hope you can understand that, can't you?"

"I do, but do me a favor, Mama. This may sting, but pick up Miguel for me. Look deep into his eyes, examine his features, especially his nose. Then tell me who you see. Who do you see when you look at him?"

Kendal's words made me nervous. I examined Miguel's features as she had asked. Even looked at his hands and feet, since his shoes were off. On the bottom of one of his feet was a birthmark.

It was in the exact same spot as the one on Brent's foot. Miguel's eyes were similar. So were his nose and brows. My heart started to pound against my chest. When my eyes shifted to Kendal, she was nodding her head.

"You rarely questioned why I didn't like him. I had my reasons, but mainly because he had raped me one day while you were gone. I was afraid of him. That's why I left for good because you refused to get rid of him. My boyfriend, Micah, is the only one who knows the truth. I thought my baby was his, but when Miguel was born, Brent was written all over him. I was crushed, but Micah is helping me raise Miguel as his son. That's all he'll ever know. I ask you to keep this secret between us because I don't want any of us to hurt anymore because of that damn Brent Carson."

I was still. My dry lips stuck together. My eyes were without a blink, and my stomach was in a knot. I wanted to scream. Wanted to cry. Wanted to run out that door and go kill Brent, but I would only get so far. My emotions were about to take over, so I handed Miguel back to Kendal. I stood and kissed them both.

"Good-bye, Kendal, and don't you ever come back here with your baby again. Thank you for sharing that with me. All I can say, again, is, I'm sorry."

I walked away, didn't dare look back. And when the guard opened the door for me, I was escorted to my cell where I slowly lay on the cold, hard bed and looked at the ceiling. I closed my eyes and could hear Eric yelling those five words at me, "*Is Brent Carson worth it?*"

Hell no, he wasn't. And in thirty-five years, I would make him pay for all of this. Then again, revenge had never been mine. There was no question in my mind that Brent's mess would catch up with him and the punishment would be dire.